Episode 1

Holly Maxwell set the photograph of the three little girls on the mantelpiece and smiled with exhausted satisfaction. Perfect. The flat, with its minimalist furnishings was ready – apart from emptying the boxes in the tiny little bedroom that was supposed to have been Isla's. Holly shrugged. All her life she had dreamed of becoming a career girl, and of sharing a flat in a big city with her two dearest friends, Isla and Jenny. Each of them had vowed to change the world: Holly would make people happy by cooking them delicious food, Jenny would be a wonderful nurse, and Isla... Isla would sing and warring factions would put down their weapons to listen to her.

Holly studied the small photograph. There she was, in the middle, one pigtail already undone and the ribbon gone. On her right stood Jenny, her hair and her blue and white uniform dress as neat as they had been in the morning, and as neat as they would be when she returned home; and on her left, Isla, so lovely with her short bouncy auburn curls which refused to grow any longer, and her large expressive eyes. Holly looked into those eyes. Had there been, even then, a slight air of anxiety?

'Don't be silly, Holly Maxwell,' she scolded herself. 'Ambitions change.'

Isla's had certainly changed. Like Holly and Jenny, she had left the farming community where their families had lived for generations, but she had not studied singing. She had chosen instead to become a primary school teacher and had returned to teach in the very school where their friendship had been forged. Too late to change career now, for she was also engaged.

Holly might not agree with her friend but she would support her. Wasn't that what friends were for after all? Besides, the man

LOVE CHANGES EVERYTHING

Childhood friends, Holly, Jenny and Isla plan to take the world by storm. Holly will be a first-class chef, Jenny a superb nurse, and Isla will become a great singer. Within a few weeks of settling into their new flat in Edinburgh, each girl has a foot firmly on the ladder of success. Everything is going according to plan until they meet three very different but very eligible men. Is it possible for them to continue with their career plans? Can they 'have it all.' Or, in fact, does Love Change Everything?

LOVE CHANGES EVERYTHING

Love Changes Everything

by

Eileen Ramsay

Dales Large Print Books
Long Preston, North Yorkshire,
BD23 4ND, England.

British Library Cataloguing in Publication Data.

Ramsay, Eileen
    Love changes everything.

    A catalogue record of this book is
    available from the British Library

    ISBN   978-1-84262-873-7 pbk

Published in Large Print 2012 by arrangement with
Eileen Ramsay

Dales Large Print is an imprint of Library Magna Books Ltd.

Printed and bound in Great Britain by
T.J. (International) Ltd., Cornwall, PL28 8RW

Isla was engaged to was Holly's own brother, Ross, one of the nicest guys anywhere. How could Holly say, 'Isla, I think you're making a mistake?'

She shook her head as if to clear it of troublesome thoughts, and turned instead to what she would do next. The strident ringing of the telephone interrupted her, and she looked around in surprise. The landline was so new that she had forgotten for the moment that they even had one.

'The hall, the hall,' she muttered, and hurried out of the kitchen to answer it.

'Holly, it's Evelyn Hammond from Fabulous Food.'

Holly felt her stomach start churning while she listened. She crossed her fingers.

'Your CV is good, and I'd like to give you a try. Of course, the only way to judge a chef is by the food he or she prepares. I know this is a short notice, but a friend has just arrived back from a tour of duty and I want to give a small dinner party for him. He says he'll be free on Saturday. Will you do the cooking?'

Holly's thoughts were tumultuous. This was the chance for which she had worked and waited. What had she planned for Saturday? Whatever it was, it would wait. She tried to make her voice smile. 'Of course, Mrs Hammond. What would you like me to serve?'

Now Evelyn Hammond displayed one of the characteristics that had made Holly want to work for her. 'It's a straightforward group – no vegetarians or special diets, and two soldiers who'll eat anything that will stay on the plate. If you choose a menu and ring me back with it, along with a list of all the ingredients, I'll buy everything you need. My husband will do the wines, so that's one less thing for you to worry about. Could you possibly let me have it tomorrow morning?'

'Certainly.' After all, Holly could hardly say, I am living out of a suitcase and some cardboard boxes. Ring me back in two weeks, as you promised.

'Thank you, Holly. I am relying on you.'

The phone call finished, Holly looked around. Somewhere in the flat there was a file of tested and successful menus. Was it unpacked? She hurried into her bedroom where there was a bookcase. It was empty! No recipe file – and she had promised Jenny something special this evening. Still, not a problem for an experienced chef.

Although Holly had always been the most academic of the three friends, she was the one who had chosen not to go to university. Her dream had always been to own her own catering company.

This evening she would prepare dinner as if she were preparing a meal – or at least a course – for her first clients. She had found lovely halibut in the fish shop round the corner. The same dish would be a perfect starter for the dinner party, and it was a recipe she could do standing on her head. A picture of herself cooking upside-down came into her head and made her laugh, lightening the tension.

She took a notebook and a pen back into

the kitchen that was now full of light from the tall window; something she loved about the flat. Right now there was only a small wooden table and two wooden chairs, not even a chair for a guest. Perhaps Jenny could look around for some. Holly wrote *Chairs* on top of her paper and began to prepare dinner.

While she prepared she jotted.

Halibut, sour cream, grated cheese, seedless grapes, dill, Tabasco.

Just writing the words and smelling the ingredients made her taste buds tingle. She noted the quantities she was using for two, and multiplied by four and a little bit more. Today she was cooking for two women, but at the party there would be, she assumed, four men and four women.

About two minutes to prepare and twenty minutes to cook.

She set the prepared dish aside. It would be perfect for Jenny after an exhausting day on the wards, and Mrs Hammond's guests would surely love it. Now to decide what to have after the fish. What would suit two soldiers? Of course, Beef Wellington.

Now she had time to look for her menus. If they were in a box of books in Isla's room she could clear one of the boxes and fill the bookshelf at the same time. Not Isla's room, she reminded herself. Isla was going to marry Ross and stay in Angus. She, Holly Maxwell, meanwhile, was going to wow Evelyn Hammond and her guests with her cooking skills. She was on her way

Jenny Grant, who had had no lunch, was sitting down in the hospital cafeteria enjoying a hot cup of tea. She had picked up a sandwich but, remembering that Holly had promised something special for dinner, had returned it.

'Have a walnut.' The voice sounded desperate.

Staff nurse Moira Stewart scraped back a chair with a hand that held a knobbly bag and sat down carefully as she lowered the mug of tea held in her other hand onto the table. 'My Jim couldn't do that, you know,' she observed. 'Move a chair, carry nuts, not spill one drop of a lifesaving brew, all at the same time. Limited creatures, men.' She smiled at Jenny who knew perfectly well that Moira loved Jim, her husband. 'Help yourself. Protein.'

Jenny dug into the bag. 'Thanks, I was hungry but Holly's cooking something special and I didn't want to spoil my appetite.'

Moira looked at her and scowled. 'Totally unfair, Jenny. You live with a gourmet cook who uses you as a guinea pig, yet there's not an extra ounce on you.' She smoothed her uniform down over her plump thighs. 'Have another, have ten. We've never had such a crop. The kids say if they never see another walnut in their lunch boxes it will be too soon. I really must learn how to preserve them.'

'I'll ask Holly.'

'Bless you.' Moira sipped her tea. 'This is bliss, isn't it? Peace and quiet.' She sat back in her chair and looked at Jenny measuringly. 'I saw you skipping off to avoid Mr Ashford.'

'Don't be silly. I just haven't had the chance of a break till now, that's all.' She would try to avoid saying any more. Moira was a good friend and a better nurse, but sometimes, especially with Jenny's non-existent love life, she was like a little terrier with a bone. The least said about Simon Ashford, one of the five consultant nephrologists here at the hospital, the better.

'I heard one of your bing-bong machines going off at regular intervals.'

She meant the dialysis machine. According to Moira, that was the noise they made when they needed attention. Several patients now referred to them in the same way. It did make them seem friendlier.

Jenny stood up, finishing her tea as she did so. 'I'd better get back to it, but I should think that Mr Ashford is quite capable of sorting it.' As senior staff nurse, Jenny was responsible for supervision of the ward and the general day-to-day care of the patients. 'If not, then any one of my nurses can help. Thanks for the nuts.'

The ward was silent except for the swishing sound of water running through the machines, and the muffled music coming from several sets of earphones. How different it had been earlier, when two emergency patients had come in at almost the same time. No wonder there had been no time for lunch.

She was annoyed to see the consultant sitting at her station, but controlled her feelings immediately. 'May I help you with something, Mr Ashford?'

Simon Ashford stumbled to his feet. He looked exhausted, and she remembered that he had actually been in the hospital during the night and then had returned for his arranged shift.

He smiled tentatively at her. 'Can't we dispense with formality when we're alone, Jenny? I know I behaved badly in Dumfries, but I've said I'm sorry.'

'And I accepted your apology.'

'But you haven't forgiven me.'

Jenny had trained in the dialysis unit of the Crichton Hospital in Dumfries, where Simon had been doing his residency. Instantly attracted to each other, they had started to date casually, but when their feelings began to grow deeper and to develop Simon had backed off, suddenly and cruelly. Jenny had been left feeling not only hurt but also embarrassed. If only he had said something, explained. Instead, without a word of farewell, he had transferred to another hospital, in Glasgow.

She had been delighted when her promotion to senior staff nurse had come through, and with it the hoped-for move to Edinburgh's magnificent new Royal Infirmary. But now, a few years later, here he was in the same hospital, and Jenny had been devastated to discover that the feelings she had had for this brilliant young man were as strong as ever.

She looked at his tired face, and considered. Had she forgiven him for making her fall in love with him and then leaving her?

'Of course I have,' she answered him now and was delighted to hear how serene she sounded. 'That was such a long time ago.'

'Jenny, please. I wanted to marry you; you know I love ... loved you. But it wouldn't have been right...'

She interrupted him. 'I have both forgotten and forgiven. But, as for informality, you know only too well what hospital gossip is like. I don't want either of us talked about. I'm sure you'd agree that it's much more professional if we stick to 'Mr Ashford' and 'Nurse Grant'. No one here need know that we were ever more than colleagues.'

'As you wish, Nurse.' He turned and walked off.

Jenny took her place at the table and, with hands that had begun to shake, skimmed through the notes that had been left for her. She raised her head once more to look down the ward and to listen for sounds, but all was calm.

Patients had to be weighed both before and after their treatment. She looked at the results from the morning session and checked them against the weights from each patient's last session. Most of them had treatment two or three times a week, and for two or three hours at a time. They were given strict dietary rules, which were relatively easy to follow – no fruit juices, no potatoes. The great life-saving machines easily spotted someone who had indulged in forbidden fruit.

Most of those in this afternoon were waiting and praying for a kidney transplant, but there were two who had had transplants that had been rejected. Jenny did not allow herself to consider how devastating that must have been. Every story in here was a tragedy, but it was better to focus on the fact that these expensive machines, gurgling away companionably, were saving lives.

Just then she heard it – bing-bong, and she got up immediately and walked quickly down the sunlit corridor between the beds on either side. She could tell at once what was amiss, and adjusted the machine, which began immediately to gurgle quietly.

'Daft machine,' the old man sitting up in the bed said querulously as Jenny adjusted it.

'It must be a man, Mr Anderson – thinks it knows best.'

Mr Anderson smiled. 'I do call him Joe, Nurse Grant. Maybe I should call it Jenny, and then it'll behave.'

'You never know. Everything all right now?'

The old man pointed to the CD-player lying on the bed beside him. 'My grandson gave me this to listen to music while I'm in here. You wouldn't know how to buzz it forward, would you?'

Jenny picked it up. 'I think so. There, it's this button.'

'Aye, but I leave my finger on too long and I miss the bits I really want to hear.'

'There you go. Just hit this.' She picked up

the CD sleeve. 'For instance, if you're trying to listen to Nessun Dorma...'

'That's actually one I want to miss.' He smiled. 'Thanks, Nurse. I think I've got it now.'

Jenny looked at her watch. 'Almost time for you and Joe to be disconnected.'

She headed back to the nurses' station, checking machines as she went and reflecting on how cheerful most of the patients were. There was a low growling sound and she patted her flat stomach, which was reminding her that it had had only a few nuts and three cups of tea since six o'clock that morning. She shrugged. It was the end of a long working day, and by the time she got home one of the best cooks in Edinburgh would be popping a dish of something delicious into the oven.

Time to disconnect the bing-bong machines.

The village hall was filling up nicely. Isla Wren peeked through the curtains and smiled as she saw her parents sitting in the middle of the front row. It was as if she were five years old again, in the infants' class, and preparing to make her debut singing 'Away in a Manger' in the school Christmas concert. This year, however, she was the teacher, not the pupil.

She peered through again, hoping to spot Ross. She couldn't see her fiancé, but his parents sat next to hers, along with Jenny's parents, the Grants. They made a strong row of support for Isla Wren.

Isla sighed. Would they always be so supportive?

She felt for the envelope in her pocket. She was filled with doubt – and some guilt, for she had told no one about what she'd done. She should have told Ross, or at least discussed it with him. But the decision had been made so quickly, and without thinking everything through and now, just as she had felt that nothing would come of it, this letter had appeared, with its message that both thrilled and terrified her.

'A kiss for luck?' She found herself swept into strong young arms and kissed thoroughly.

'Ross, you shouldn't.' She was flustered and a little embarrassed.

He laughed and kissed her again, but lightly, on the tip of her nose. 'Holly says you're to break a leg.'

Holly, Jenny and Isla. The three musketeers, as Mr Maxwell had called them. 'She's too busy to come home.' Ross looked down at his fiancée and a troubled doubt shadowed his fresh face. 'You're absolutely sure you don't wish you'd found a job in Edinburgh with the others? That you're happy in the country?'

He seemed ill-at ease somehow, not his usual confident self...

She smiled. 'Of course I am.'

But, even as she answered him doubt struck her. Was this the right time to show him the letter? Oh, why was everything so difficult?

She tried to pull away from him. 'I've got to go; I'll see you at supper time.'

'Isla?'

'What's wrong?'

'Nothing.' He shook his head. 'Something has come up, but we can talk later. I just worry that you might long for the bright lights?'

'I don't.' That much was true. 'I have to sing, sweetheart.' Why had she said that? She had meant to say, 'I have to go.'

The concert began: one item followed another, each received well by the supportive audience. Ross Maxwell didn't join his parents, but stood alone at the back of the hall, his handsome face giving away none of his confused thoughts. He listened to each of the singers and the verse speakers; he whistled and stamped his feet as he applauded the highland dancers and the school choir. But he was interested in only one performer, Isla.

He had been listening to his sister's friend sing since she was three years old, but it had never really occurred to him that Isla's voice was out of the ordinary, as there were many good voices in the farming community. Her father had a grand voice, heard in the Kirk every Sunday.

'Isla's? Aye, it's a bonnie voice, but man, you should hae heard my granny,' Mr Wren would reminisce when people told him how beautifully his daughter sang.

Tonight Ross heard Isla sing some Scottish songs, always a big favourite with the audience, and then *Oh, Holy Night*, a fearsomely difficult carol. Her clear sweet voice rang round the old village hall, a hall that had heard her father, her grandmother, and even her renowned great-grandmother before her.

'My Isla,' he thought. 'My lovely, lovely Isla.'

She finished to rapturous applause and even some foot stamping, which could not be good for the hall's ancient wooden floors.

It was time for an intermission. An enticing selection of sandwiches, scones, and other home-baking was revealed on the large trestle tables that stretched along one wall. Ross peeled himself off the wall and walked forward, but was caught up in the surge of people and, good-naturedly, stepped back.

'Penny for them?'

Isla was there, smiling.

'I was just thinking...' He changed his mind about what he had been about to say 'that you could do with a cup of tea.'

He went off to fetch it and Isla stood and received the congratulations for her own performance and for that of the children. For this end-of-term concert she had put together a choir from the whole school, not just her own class.

'The bairns will lift the trophy at the festival next year, Isla. They've never been better.'

That sentiment was expressed several times in different ways.

Would she be there at the festival? Again she reached for the envelope in her pocket, then turned with relief as Ross rescued her from proud parents and boisterous children.

'I brought us a bit of shortbread. There'll

be nothing left when your choir is through eating.' He pointed to the table where apparently starving children were greedily filling their plates.

They moved to the doorway leading into the kitchen, where a thick curtain would give them a little privacy. Hidden by the curtain, he lifted her hand to his lips and gently kissed it. 'I need to talk to you, love.'

Isla's heart began to beat faster. 'Ross? Has something happened?'

'Not exactly,' he began, and then he stopped. 'I've been offered immediate tenancy of a farm. Just a small one – a hundred and fifty acres – but there's a house, bigger than our cottage.'

Isla thought of the cottage on Ross's father's farm that they had been renovating and redecorating. It would be ready by the summer, and by then this dream would be out of her system. 'Where is it?'

'Aberdeenshire?'

'Aberdeenshire.' She repeated the word as if it was some far-off place, instead of just an hour or so up the road. 'Immediate? You would have to live on the farm?'

'Aye. But what an opportunity. I have to go for it, Isla.'

The envelope in her skirt pocket began to feel heavier and heavier. 'Ross, we can't discuss our future here, like this.'

He kept her hand in his. 'I've thought of nothing else all day. I need to do this but I want you with me.'

He held her away from him and looked down into her troubled eyes. 'You'll have to give in your notice, Isla, and I know that'll break your heart. But I think we should get married at Christmas. Won't that be wonderful? OK, it won't be the big wedding we'd planned – there isn't time. But you can still have a lovely dress and Holly and Jenny as bridesmaids, all the wee trimmings. Will you do it, Isla? Will you bring forward our wedding day?'

It was raining that Saturday morning, but Holly refused to allow the rain to affect her mood. This was her big chance. Everything must go well; the food had to be absolute perfection.

She had left early, determined to walk part of the way and to arrive with a clear uncluttered mind. She was still surprised daily by the beauty of this capital city, Edinburgh, and was sure that she would never tire of it, even in the rain. 'Look up, look up.' She wanted to alert other walkers to the glories of the buildings, or the great castle standing guard there on the hill. But most people seemed to hurry to their destinations with eyes firmly fixed on the ground beneath their feet.

Holly liked walking in the rain. The storm that had raged all night had worn itself out, and showers were light and intermittent. She was wearing a long raincoat and her favourite pink Wellington boots, and had to resist the urge to stamp in puddles, especially in the New Town. The thought of frosty dowagers frowning at her through their high Georgian windows made her laugh and she arrived in Great King Street in an upbeat mood.

Evelyn Hammond had everything ready for her. 'Make yourself a sandwich and a fresh pot of coffee. Help yourself to anything you need.' She showed Holly the kitchen and pantries and made sure that none of her equipment was unfamiliar to her chef.

'By the way,' she added just as the family were leaving, 'Primrose's godfather may arrive before we get back. Just let him in, please, and he'll make himself at home.'

The hours sped by. Holly had no difficulty in finding her way around the streamlined and thoroughly up-to-date kitchen. Preparing the three-course meal was no problem, as generous quantities of everything she had asked for were set out on tabletops and in a refrigerator.

House telephones sounded at intervals, but the answering machine took care of them. Then, just before four, Holly's own mobile phone rang. Her hands were deep in a bowl of pastry which she finished kneading it before she answered.

'Can you talk for a minute?' It was Jenny.

'I'm preparing Beef Wellington, but it can sit for a minute. Have you found something?'

'Two chairs, more dining-room than kitchen. We can put them in the hall. I also saw a superb sideboard, but I want you to see it first.'

Holly looked at her floury hands and the succulent beef sitting on a marble board. 'Can't be done.'

'Never mind.' Jenny was silent for a moment. 'Holly, there's just one other thing. Isla rang. She's had a fight with Ross. She wants to come and spend the night with us, but she's not sure how you'll feel.'

'Because she's had a fight with my brother? Tell her not to be silly.'

'I did say that, but I think there's more to it.'

The doorbell rang before Holly could reply. She told Jenny that she would talk to her later and, after casting an anguished look at her unprepared main course, she hurried to the front door.

A tall, distinguished man was standing on the doorstep. He was almost the stereotypical country gentleman, dressed in tweeds and a well-worn Barbour jacket. 'You must be Holly.' He held out his hand. 'Hugh Crawford.'

Holly shook the hand that was held out to her. It was very strong, very firm, and, since she was a cook and always aware of fingernails, she noted that it was also well manicured. 'Mr Crawford, may I help you?'

'It would be nice if I could come in.' He gestured towards the door with an overnight bag.

Holly stared at him for a second before realisation struck, and she blushed to the roots of her hair. 'I'm so sorry, Mr Crawford,' she said. 'You are...'

'Primrose's godfather,' he supplied, following her in and closing the door. 'But you were quite right to make sure. I'll take this to the guest-room.' He sniffed appreciatively. 'Wonderful smells.'

He took the stairs two at a time.

'Well fit,' Holly murmured reverting to teenage slang, and she hurried back to her kitchen wondering about the existence of a Mrs Crawford. She would most likely be svelte and sophisticated, tweeds and Labradors by day and silks and pearls by night. Strangely enough, Holly found the picture she had created rather depressing.

The time flew past. Holly refused to allow herself to think about Isla or Ross. Today was important. She had to do well. Because her future depended on the success of this meal, she was more nervous than she had ever been. Evelyn's kitchen had obviously been designed for a woman who loved to cook but who also wanted her family and friends around her while she did so. It was quite contemporary, all black granite and natural wood, with a family eating area.

What I could do with a kitchen like this, Holly thought as Hugh Crawford walked into the kitchen.

He was dressed for dinner and looked just as comfortable in a dinner jacket and a blinding white evening shirt as he had looked in his tweeds. Holly, trying to stuff a large pink shrimp into a tiny tomato, looked up at him. 'Yes.' Nerves made her voice unwelcoming.

'Would you mind if I made some coffee. I spent the entire morning arguing with two rams. I know that sounds odd, but it's true, and they were unbelievably belligerent rams.'

Holly, daughter of a sheep farmer, raised her eyebrows. She had fiddly canapés to make for eight people and time was running out.

'I know you're busy, so probably you could use a cup, too.'

Holly looked down at the tiny cherry tomatoes and waved a shrimp in his direction. 'I would kill for a cup, Mr Crawford.'

'Hopefully not with a shrimp.' He smiled.

Holly smiled back – who could resist such charm? A few minutes later Holly was offered a cup of fragrant coffee.

'Sit down. Miss Maxwell.' His tone was that of a man used to giving orders, and having them obeyed. 'Obviously you have everything under control.'

She took the cup with a murmured word of thanks, and sipped gratefully. It was almost six thirty, and the guests would be arriving soon. Where were the host and hostess?

'Evelyn rang,' he said as if he had read her thoughts. 'They'll be here within the next half hour. Plenty of time. Relax and drink your coffee.'

'Thank you, Mr Crawford,' she said and tried not to think of all the things she had to do.

'It's Hugh. Right, I'll take mine off to the drawing room and play butler if the doorbell rings. But it won't, not for some time.'

She watched him go, noting the straight back and the broad shoulders. If there had been time she would have enjoyed chatting with him about farming and the eccentricities of rams.

Silly Holly. You're hired help, she scolded herself, and returned to the cheeseboard.

Five exhausting hours later she was placing the last dishes into the dishwasher. Everything had gone smoothly, and the guests seemed happy with the food, as very little had been left on the plates.

'Oh, Holly, you didn't have to do that.' Evelyn Hammond, in a wine-coloured velvet evening skirt and a glorious, pale pink, lace blouse, had come into the kitchen. 'I have a girl coming to wash up tomorrow morning. I should have told you.' She gave Holly no time to answer but went on. 'Do have a glass of wine and some food. I've ordered a taxi for you. We'll be here for hours yet.'

She whirled out again.

Holly closed the door of the dishwater and sat down at the table. Bone-tired, she wanted neither wine nor food.

There had been no, 'Well done, Holly' or 'That was magnificent, Holly.'

She had no idea what Evelyn Hammond thought of her cooking or what her chances were of being asked to work for the prestigious caterer.

A few minutes later she heard the doorbell that told her the taxi had arrived, and as she left she heard murmurs from the drawing-room and then a man's deep laugh. She knew that it was Hugh Crawford, and sighed. She had heard him laugh earlier, when she had been clearing the first course. Had he informed Evelyn Hammond that her trainee chef had been more nervous than a beginner?

'Even if he did, surely the meal impressed them,' she told herself as the taxi bore her through the lovely but much quieter city.

Jenny was still awake when Holly let herself in quietly. Isla was asleep on the sofa, a blanket draped over her. Holly looked down at her friend's swollen eyelids and then at Jenny, who didn't look too happy either.

'You two look as bad as I feel,' she murmured to Jenny.

'Didn't your meal go well?'

'No idea. They ate everything, so I

suppose it was all right.' This was not the time to look for sympathy. 'Hello,' she began as Isla stirred. 'How do you like the flat?'

Isla's tear-stained face looked up at her. 'I've done something absolutely awful. You'll hate me?'

Jenny went off to make cocoa, and Holly sat down beside her brother's fiancée. 'You slugged the head teacher?'

'Don't be silly.' Isla reached into her dressing gown pocket and handed Holly a rather damp envelope. 'I auditioned for a place with a semi-professional opera company. I didn't tell anyone, not even Ross. Wouldn't you say that was deceitful?'

Holly wasn't listening, being too busy reading the letter. She looked up, her eyes shining. 'But this is wonderful, Isla – you've got it.' She was surprised to see that Isla looked set to cry again. 'I'm thrilled for you. Isn't it marvellous, Jenny?'

Jenny put down the tray with its three mugs. 'Ross doesn't think so. She's given him back his ring.'

Episode 2

'Isla's given Ross back his ring,' Jenny said. Her words echoed around the room.

Holly looked at her best friend and then at her brother's fiancée. Never in a million years would she have imagined this.

'But why?' She held out the letter. 'You're not telling me he wasn't pleased you passed the audition?'

Isla started to weep again in earnest, and Jenny put her arms around Holly and led her out of the room. At the door she looked over her shoulder. 'Try to pull yourself together, Isla, while I make us all some nice, hot cocoa.'

In the kitchen Holly sat down, exhausted and dejected. What on earth was happening? She was almost too tired to think.

'Nurse Grant to the rescue,' Jenny said.

'I'll bet you were too busy to eat.'

'Food's the last thing on my mind.'

'We'll see.' Jenny started preparing toast, buttered and spread with honey. 'Take off your coat and boots. Wellies are definitely not kitchen wear!'

'Don't worry,' she went on. 'Isla will tell us both everything, and then we can think, together, as we always have done about the really big things.'

So it proved. Jenny sat her two friends down and put the tray of food in front of them. She smiled gently as she watched Isla, who had sworn tearfully that food would choke her, eat a thick slice of sticky toast and wash it down with cocoa.

Holly merely nibbled, but did finish her hot drink.

Isla blew her nose once more on a tissue, gulped once or twice and began. 'First you must believe that I love Ross very much, and I want to be his wife. It's just, oh, it sounds so silly, but the desire to sing just seems to be growing stronger and stronger inside me. Is it so selfish to want both – Ross and the farm plus the chance to sing?'

Her friends looked at her, Jenny encouragingly and Holly with no expression at all, but neither spoke.

'You see, I've never really been sure that I have a great voice – me, Isla Wren, a shepherd's daughter from Angus. And then there was Ross.' She looked up into Holly's eyes for the first time. 'I think I have been in love with Ross since I was little. When he said he loved me, I was sure that marriage to him was the right thing to do.'

'Yet six months before your wedding day you applied for an audition with an opera company.' Holly spoke at last.

Isla stood up, walked to the window and looked out at the lashing rain. 'It was just there – the ad, in the newspaper. I hardly knew what I was doing when I filled it in, but I do know that I wasn't hopeful. They'll laugh at me, I decided, and then at least I'll be content. Because they'll know the difference between a nice voice and a great voice.'

'But why didn't you tell Ross?' Holly was on her feet now, too, and the friends stared at each other across the pretty room.

'Probably because she thought that, if she told him she was auditioning for an opera company, he would think she didn't really want to settle down with him. Also, being our Isla, she had no doubt convinced herself that she would fail the audition, and so why upset Ross, if it wasn't necessary?' Jenny, staring into the remains of her cocoa, spoke for her friend. 'And if – when – they rejected her, she could let this wee dream go back to sleep. Am I right, Isla?'

Isla came back to sit down again. She nodded. 'They came to Aberdeen to listen to us – nineteen sopranos, from the hills and glens, from wee villages and big towns. We sang, they said thank you, and I left. I walked to the art gallery to look at some projects for my class, and that was that.'

'But then this letter came.' Holly waved the letter again but this time she was smiling. 'I am so proud of you, Isla.'

'It's really only for another audition.'

'What about Ross? Was he furious?'

Isla resorted to another tissue. 'He was wonderful, because he *is* wonderful. It came at the wrong time, though.' She told them about the offer of the farm tenancy.

'He must take it; it's an unbelievable opportunity for a young farmer. But it must be done now, and it was all just too much for me – changing the wedding date, not about to be living in the lovely little cottage we'd been renovating, handing in my notice...' She shook her head. 'I just panicked and handed back his ring.'

Her friends nodded sympathetically.

'When's the audition?' Holly asked.

'Wednesday.'

'Right. You're welcome to stay here on Tuesday night.' She looked at Jenny for confirmation. 'But for now I think we're all exhausted and need to go to bed.'

Holly did not want to leave the flat on Sunday. They had slept late, apart from

Jenny, who had got up quietly and, with her usual minimum of fuss, had made herself breakfast before leaving for the hospital.

The smell of percolating coffee eventually penetrated Holly's sleep, and she got up and stumbled into the kitchen, where she found a very woebegone Isla. 'Giving back the ring was such an over-reaction. Do you think he'll ever forgive me?'

Holly, who had been head-over-heels in love with a talented pastry chef in Vienna until she discovered that, as well as swearing undying affection for her, he'd also been involved with a very pretty Italian waitress, felt strongly that she was not the person to answer this question. 'Go home and talk to him.'

She took the mug of coffee that Isla handed her. 'Have you decided to miss the audition?'

Isla's face was white and set. 'After causing all this trouble? No. Oh, Holly, why can't I have this chance and Ross too?'

Holly sipped her reviving coffee appreciatively. 'Women have been making com-promises about having it all since the beginning of time, but I know Ross, and I think he's fairly good at compromise, too.'

Immediately Isla looked happier. 'He is perfect, isn't he?'

'No,' Ross's wee sister said. 'No one is.' She looked at the oven clock. 'I'm off to have a shower. I'll take you down to Waverley when you're ready to go back.'

Holly carried her mobile phone with her to the railway station. If Evelyn Hammond rang the flat and got no reply, she might just decide to try the mobile number. But the phone stayed silent as she shepherded Isla around the newly refurbished station, and no cheery little red light was winking at her from the answering machine when she returned to the flat.

The families of the two young people had naturally decided not to discuss the events, and since Holly knew that her mother would be unable to talk to her daughter without bringing up the broken engagement, she avoided ringing home. It was a miserable Sunday, not helped by the weather.

By the time the house telephone did ring, on Monday afternoon, Holly had been considering what other job options might be available to her.

'You want me to start immediately?' She could scarcely take it in.

'Of course. You were never in any doubt, were you?' Evelyn Hammond laughed. 'The food was wonderful. All my guests said so. Hugh especially was singing your praises. So, when can you start?'

Holly's heart was soaring when she put the telephone down. She had the job of her dreams, and Hugh Crawford had liked her food. Not, she decided, that that mattered. Hugh Crawford was merely an army friend of her new employer, home on leave. She would probably never see him again. She shrugged and went off to make soup, always a very fulfilling exercise.

Tuesday was busy but enjoyable. Holly met

the two other full-time chefs who worked for Fabulous Foods, the kitchen staff and one or two of the waitresses. For a big event Evelyn used agency waiters, but her company was now so busy that she was able to hire waiting staff as full-time employees.

Evelyn explained how she sourced her food, informing her that as much as possible was bought locally. 'Tomorrow we're doing a ladies' luncheon at a lovely home in Ramsay Gardens. The house itself is quite large but the kitchen is tiny, so we'll do most of the preparation here. Ladies tend to like light food but they love spectacular desserts, which Boris will make and complete here. Wait till you see his spun-sugar creations! I've always threatened to wear one as a hat. No-one would know – until it started melting.'

Working with Evelyn was going to be fun, Holly decided with a happy quiver of excitement, but it was also going to be extremely hard work. Her clients were demanding. They knew the best and expected to receive it.

'I want you to do the soup, Holly, and the vegetarian option. We've had two orders, but make enough for four please. There's always someone who sees the vegetarian option and must have it. Always make more than you think you'll need; the firm's reputation is at stake.'

The chefs worked in peaceful harmony. Boris Minsky, the pastry chef, had very little to say, but every time Holly looked in his direction, he smiled. It was he who made coffee and provided delicious shortbread biscuits when they took a well-earned rest. Nora Glover, on the other hand, more than made up for the Ukrainian's silence, but her chatter seemed not to get in the way of her work.

'I'm a good plain cook,' she told Holly proudly when they were enjoying their coffee. 'Can't do the fancy stuff – a cheery tomato and a bit of parsley are about all I can produce by way of garnish. Not like Boris here. Don't get too close to him when he's spinning sugar or Lord knows how you'll end up.'

Boris grunted and smiled, but did not rise to the bait, and soon they got back to work. Holly roasted peppers of all colours, peeling off the roasted skin to expose the succulent flesh that she then diced, ready to mix with the other prepared ingredients. At three o'clock she began to prepare her vegetarian dish, a medley of beans, pulses, vegetable and cheese.

She had a nasty moment when she saw that the beans needed for it would have to be soaked overnight before cooking, which meant she would be way behind tomorrow.

She looked around frantically, wondering how to gain entry to this kitchen in the early morning. Did this signal the end of her career already?

'Problem, Holly?' Boris had noticed her nervousness.

'My beans...' she began.

'On the stove. Not like Evelyn not to say. No matter. Turn on now, and they will be

49

ready in few hours.'

Mastering a desire to throw her arms around Boris's neck, she thanked him as calmly as she could manage and hurried over to the stove. Glad that her heart rate seemed to be slowing down, she prepared the rest of the ingredients.

She was exhausted when she got home, but her own pot of thick, nourishing soup was simmering away, thanks to Jenny, who had also made up a bed for Isla.

When Isla arrived, the flatmates saw that her fingers were still ringless. 'I haven't spoken to Ross,' she said, noticing their hastily averted glances. 'He's gone up to Aberdeen to arrange his tenancy. But tell us all about your first day, Holly. There's been more than enough talk about me.'

On Wednesday, Jenny went to pick up the two chairs she had bought at the antiques shop on Saturday. It had stopped raining, and Stockbridge was at its best in the winter sunshine. Jenny loved shopping in the area;

there were so many lovely shops and boutiques. Some she would enter, while others were definitely not in her budget. Though she loved looking in the cleverly-dressed windows.

The owner of Vazana's Antiques had served her himself. 'I'm giving these away,' he'd said as he dealt with her cheque. 'Edwardian, you know, from – and he tapped his nose – a very good home. I hate to let them go, but I feel the same with all my beautiful things. Did you say you wanted the sideboard too?'

She gave serious consideration to popping into a coffee shop, but decided instead to find a taxi that would carry her beautiful new chairs back to the flat before the rush hour. She raised her arm as she saw a taxi approaching, but instead a large, powerful car pulled up beside her.

'At your service, Nurse Grant.'

Jenny felt her face flush scarlet. 'I was calling that taxi,' she said angrily as the cab sailed past.

'I'm available, and I'm cheaper,' Simon

Ashford pointed out.

'I can't possibly ask you to...' she began, but he was already out of the car.

'Lovely chairs. I've bought from old Vazana, too. Did you get his "I hate to let my children go" tale of woe? Half the fun of haggling with him is to hear him in action. But he knows his antiques. Hop in?'

Since her chairs were now lying on the back seat of his car, she allowed him to help her in. He waved apologetically to two women drivers behind who were being held up by his car, and Jenny saw one of them smile at him. A handsome man with a handsome car is forgiven everything, she thought angrily, and was embarrassed when he seemed to read her mind.

'Not my fault, Jenny, and courtesy costs nothing.'

'I doubt they'd have been happy to wait so long for me.'

He smiled at her again, infuriating her still further, and pulled out smoothly into the busy road. He said nothing, concentrating on the road, and Jenny found herself with no idea what to say. 'This is kind of you' sounded banal. Besides, she was angry, and had no desire to thank Simon Ashford for anything. It was enough that she had to work alongside him.

She relaxed into the smooth leather upholstery and stared out at the shop windows, lulled into a dreaming state.

'Do taxi drivers help up the stairs with chairs?'

Jenny was so surprised by the question that she turned round in the seat to look straight at his impeccable profile. 'What?'

'Just wondered. I suppose he might be given a bigger tip, but then there's the question of industry regulations.'

'"I'd help you, Missus, but it's me back – the boss won't allow it." Those kind of regulations?'

'Absolutely.'

Jenny smiled. They used to talk nonsense like this all the time. But that was before, she reminded herself.

'How do you know where you're going?'

'I don't. I assumed that, eventually, you say something like 'turn right at the next intersection and it's the third on your left.'

Tersely she directed him to their building in Morningside. 'You don't need to carry the chairs upstairs. I'm perfectly capable.'

'Indeed you are,' he said, and lapsed into a silence that was no longer companionable.

Angry with herself now for being so prickly, she was glad when he found a parking place close to the tall grey building where she and Holly had bought their lovely flat.

When she tried to take the chairs from him he shook his head. 'Don't be silly.'

He strode past her to the door, and she was forced to trot along beside him as she fished her key from her purse. She held the door open and he brushed past her, carrying the dining-room chairs very carefully.

'Which floor?'

'Top,' she murmured apologetically, but he merely started climbing. As she watched him, she felt a desire to giggle as, in her ear, she could hear Holly's voice. 'Well fit.'

She controlled herself with an effort, and reached the door just ahead of him. Part of her wanted very much to ask him to come inside, to have coffee, to talk and laugh as they had done when they worked together in Dumfries. But that was all in the past.

He seemed to understand what was going on in her head. 'Hurry up and open the door. I'm already late for my squash match, and I'm on duty this evening.'

She opened the door wide and he stepped across the threshold, placing the chairs down just inside.

'Lovely flat, Jenny,' he said. 'See you.'

Jenny stood for a moment listening to his shoes clattering on the stone steps, and then she went in and closed the door behind her.

The beautiful Usher Hall was huge, and much more frightening than the Festival Theatre where the auditions were supposed to have been held. Till this moment, Isla had thought she was calm and controlled, and looking forward to the experience. After all, she told herself firmly, she had got through the first round.

The telephone call she'd received before eight o'clock in the morning, however, had completely thrown her off balance. The venue had been changed. They were very sorry but could she find her way to the Usher Hall for eleven o'clock! The Usher Hall where had appeared the world's greatest singers, the most brilliant pianists, violinists and conductors.

Nervously, Isla went to twist her engagement ring around on her finger. But, of course, it was not there, and at that realisation something seemed to drop down to the pit of her stomach and lie there, a large, heavy lump. She felt tears start in her eyes, and took a deep breath to control herself.

There were two other girls in the green room, waiting to be called. To Isla they appeared unbelievably sophisticated. Both of them had been present in Aberdeen but she had not spoken to them there; this time there were just the three of them and they drank coffee and tried to make conversation.

One, a tall, rather glamorous girl, had already sung small roles with several major companies and Isla envied her apparent serenity. The other was not as nervous as Isla unless, Isla decided, she was a better actress than Isla and hid it well.

To her consternation Isla was called first, but as she found her way to the stage she consoled herself with the knowledge that, for her, the agonising wait would soon be over.

The rehearsal pianist sat at his piano on the stage and, after she had given him her music, Isla positioned herself centre stage. She could feel her knees shaking and prayed that the judges would not see them from their seats in the auditorium.

The great hall was not brightly lit. The stage was bright, possibly so that the singer could be seen clearly, but the judges seemed to prefer the safer semi-darkness. One of the judges stood up, but not to speak to the trembling Isla. She called something and a voice answered from the gods, the seats almost up in the great dome, and Isla realised that someone was listening from up there too. Would he even hear her?

Feeling that she must look like a Munchkin left over from "The Wizard of Oz", Isla was suddenly pleased that Holly had suggested that she wear high-heeled boots with her short skirt. At least this Munchkin would appear to be two inches taller than she actually was.

'When you're ready, Miss Wren,' came a voice, and Isla looked over at the pianist. She had chosen to sing the hauntingly beautiful – and difficult "Countess's Aria" from Mozart's opera "The Marriage of Figaro", and just before she sang the first note she had a moment to wonder if she should have chosen something written for a younger singer. Too late, too late. She lost herself in the sublime music and sang. When she finished there was such a silence that all the doubts came flying back. But the judges said nothing, and so she counted to ten and nodded to the pianist.

Her second piece had been chosen for Ross and her parents. It might be the first and last time she would grace this hallowed stage but, for her father, she would sing the lovely Scottish song "Dream Angus."

Silence again. The two judges in the stalls seemed merely to be lying back in their comfortable chairs. Isla was too cowed to look up, but stood quaking in her boots until a disembodied voice said, 'Thank you, Miss Wren.'

She remembered to thank the pianist and then walked off into the wings, where she found herself trembling so much that she had to hold on to something until she was in control enough to find her way back to the green room.

The second singer had already been called, and the third was now too nervous to do anything but smile tentatively at Isla, who sat wondering if she was supposed merely to pick up her coat and leave. After a strained silence the second singer returned, joyful. 'It was fabulous. They seemed really, really pleased. Your turn, Frieda, they don't want to hang about.'

Isla got up and made to follow the third girl. 'I need a little air. Do you know ... are we supposed to wait? This is my first time, you see.'

'Usually everyone waits. What did they say to you?'

'Nothing, not a word.'

The girl looked sad. 'Oh, dear. I've never been at an audition were they didn't at least say thank you.'

Isla gulped. 'Someone did say thank you ... eventually.'

The other singer stood up. 'You look awful. Go outside and take a few deep breaths. After all, even if you haven't done well, you need to leave a good impression on the judges. You never know when you might meet one or other of them again.' She smiled. 'Go on. Believe me, dear, they'll find you if they want you.'

Afraid that she was going to be sick, Isla hurried out.

Boris drove Holly to Ramsay Gardens on the Wednesday morning. She was impressed by the little van, which was equipped with the latest equipment for carrying casseroles, pots full of soup, and fragile desserts without ever spilling a drop.

'Fantastic.' Holly declared as they turned right off the Royal Mile and looked out over the glorious 'Athens of the North'. It was a cold, clear day and there was a biting wind that, up here above the city, seemed to find every exposed inch of skin even in the warm catering van.

Wordlessly, Boris pulled into the parking slot they had been allocated for unloading. 'Fantastic,' Boris echoed. 'But me, I talk about my driving. See – not one drop spilled. Fantastic, no?'

So Boris had a sense of humour under that taciturn demeanour.

'Fantastic, yes,' she agreed.

Laden with boxes, they climbed the steps to the red and white house.

'These houses always make me think they've escaped from London or Bath.'

'Nothing wishes to escape from Bath, Holly. London now.' He shrugged as the door opened and their customer smiled a welcome.

While Boris finished unloading the van, Holly made herself familiar with the small but perfectly designed kitchen. She noted that there were three, obviously original, wooden stairs leading to the dining room.

'I'm glad I'm not carrying the hot soup upstairs.'

'No problem for our waiters.' Boris unveiled his glorious creations. 'Donald, the head waiter, he will do the wines. You don't need worry about nothing.'

So it proved. Holly's first real job for Fabulous Foods was a tremendous success. The hostess and her sophisticated guests were loud in their praise, not only of Boris's spectacular desserts but also of all the other dishes. One guest even sent a note to the kitchen asking if the chef would reveal the secret of the roasted pepper soup.

'What do you say, Boris?' Holly asked, flustered.

'Easy. "Thank you, Madame, but the recipes belong to Fabulous Foods." Let them argue with Evelyn.'

The recipe actually belonged to Holly, but she was quite content to have Mrs Hammond field all requests.

'Think, Holly.'

Boris pointed out later as he expertly negotiated the Edinburgh traffic. 'Your recipes are cash in the bank. You want to give them away?'

'Of course not.'

Holly smiled at him, and idly wondered about his history. He was Ukrainian, so he said, and there was no doubt that he was a superb pastry chef. His English sounded comical, since he spoke with an accent that was west coast mixed with Russian. Was he married? He wore no ring, but that meant nothing. Where had he trained? He could not have become such a magician without expert instruction.

It was, she decided, none of her business, and she sat back and relaxed while he drove. Things forgotten came back into her head. Isla and Ross. Tonight, come what may, she would speak to her parents. She crossed her fingers surreptitiously, though whether she was hoping that Isla had passed the audition or that she had failed it, she couldn't say. Poor Ross, all alone in a big house in Aberdeenshire that he did not know. Ross, her big brother, tenant of a farm.

She struggled home on the bus laden with leftovers. The delighted hostess in the gracious Old Town house had been happy for Holly and Boris to take away the extra portions.

'I know I've paid for it,' she had said lightly, 'but what would I do with it all? We eat out almost every night, and I never eat lunch at home unless I'm entertaining. Do give it to the staff.'

'Perks of the job,' Boris had told Holly. 'Sometimes we barely have a crust of bread left. But other times, ladies' lunches make good suppers.'

There was none of Holly's vegetarian option left, or of Boris's spun sugar creations, but Holly was going home with chicken enough for three.

Jenny let her in, talking the carrier bag and the casserole dish from her. 'I'll put these in the kitchen,' she said. 'Go and admire our new chairs. Isla's lying down on my bed with a stonking headache.'

Jenny hoped that mention of Isla would prevent Holly asking how she's managed to get the chairs up the flights of stairs and into the flat. She was correct. Holly duly admired the chairs, but then immediately wanted to know the result of the audition.

'No idea. Useless to ask Isla right now. Let's have a cup of tea and heat up all that yummy food. The aroma should bring her round. She had no breakfast, and I'm quite sure she was too tense to eat lunch either.

'Tell me about your first lunch party,' she ordered as she began to heat the chicken. 'Shall we have this with bread and a salad?'

Holly speared a slice of fresh pineapple and put it on a plate just as Isla, in her dressing-gown, joined them. 'Isla, fantastic. Tell us all. How did it go? Did they tell you, or will they call?'

Isla put her hands over her ears in mock agony at her friend's ringing tones.

'Sorry.' Holly almost whispered. 'Have a nice cup of tea. I won't say another word until you're ready.'

'I ran away,' Isla whispered. 'It was awful.'

Holly and Jenny froze in the middle of preparing supper. 'Awful?' they asked together.

'I sang and no one said anything, not a word. And this experienced singer told me that they always say something – 'Thank you for coming' or something like that. She said I should go outside and get some air, and that they'd come for me if they wanted

66

me. But no one came.'

'Oh, Isla.' Holly took her friend in her arms. 'I'm so sorry.'

'But surely...' began Jenny just as the house telephone rang. Since she was closest she went to answer it, calling back over her shoulder, 'That'll be them now.'

Jenny and Isla watched as she listened, then turned. 'Sorry, Isla. It's for you, Jenny. Mrs Hammond.'

Wondering what she could have done wrong, Holly rushed to the telephone.

'Holly, so sorry to bother you, but are you free on Sunday afternoon?'

'Yes, Evelyn. Can I help you with something?'

'It's not for me, dear. I'll be a guest. Major Crawford wants to have a luncheon for sixteen at his home near Lanarkshire – a ghastly old keep with a rotten kitchen and inadequate plumbing. He hopes you'll do the whole thing. I should be furious, of course.' She laughed. 'What do you say? Will you do it?'

Holly's heart skipped a beat as she remembered the tall, elegant man with the deep laugh. Did she want to see him again – and perhaps meet his wife too? She took a deep breath and spoke quietly into the receiver. Then she turned to her friends.

'What is a keep, exactly?'

Episode 3

'Miss Maxwell, I'm very pleased that you're able to do this lunch party – hardly fair to ask Evelyn to do an event at which she's a guest.'

Holly's heart, which had been pounding with excitement, dived into the pit of her stomach at Hugh Crawford's words and lay there like a stone. She shook herself mentally. For one mad moment she had thought that her cooking skills had won her a first customer. But they had in a way. After all, Evelyn must have recommended her.

'Of course. I'd be delighted, since it seems to be fine with Mrs Hammond.'

She hoped he hadn't noticed a delay in her answer.

'She tells me you hope to have your own firm one day.'

There was another pause and Holly realised that he was waiting for her to say something.

'Yes,' she said. 'I do.' Holly Maxwell, brilliant cook and conversationalist.

She cleared her throat. 'What type of meal had you in mind, Major?'

'I hoped that you would advise me. Apart from Evelyn and Gregor, her husband, we're all soldiers – and wives and partners, of course. I want something delicious but not your typical British Sunday lunch. We could have that at the Mess.'

'So no roast beef and Yorkshire pud, then? Followed by the most divine apple pie, with a French twist?

He laughed. 'Tempting. I love apple pie,

with any kind of twist. You worked in France, didn't you? We must chat about it some time. Could you perhaps do something French, but not classical? Oh, and it has to be hot. You do know that I live in rather a tumbledown, sixteenth century keep, don't you? What passes for our central heating is very unreliable.' He hesitated for a moment and then continued ruefully. 'The ovens don't always behave either.'

Unreliable ovens and dodgy central heating. Thank goodness *le roast beef* was off the menu. 'I'll manage. Something piping hot and tasty, in fact, with a whiff of France, but not classic French cuisine.'

'Got it.'

'I'll get back to you, Major, with some ideas.'

'Wonderful. In fact, I'm at the Castle for meetings tomorrow. Edinburgh Castle, that is. You're not free for coffee, are you, latish in the day?'

Her first business meeting. 'Around six would be good.'

'Fine. Could you meet me at Eco Vino on Cockburn Street? They do great hot salads there, and the coffee's good. Great watch-the-world-go-by window tables too. Sorry, you probably know it – all young Edinburgh entrepreneurs seem to.'

'I don't know it, but it sounds great.' She rather enjoyed being called an entrepreneur. One day, perhaps. She crossed her fingers for luck. A first client with his own castle – for that was how Isla had described a keep. She felt quite excited at the idea of visiting the keep, and perhaps learning something of its history.

She retrieved her wandering mind, once again agreed to meet and hung up, vowing to herself that she would create a meal that neither Major Hugh Crawford nor his guests would ever forget.

On her way to the station Isla alighted from the bus near The Usher Hall. She had not really taken it in yesterday – wee Isla Wren from an Angus glen, singing where the greatest singers the world had ever known had sung before her. She stood in front of the Sheraton Hotel and looked across the busy Lothian Road at the magnificent concert hall, once again feeling small and insignificant. 'I actually stood on the stage in there and sang,' she told herself in wonder. Then it really hit her; she had done it. The telephone call had come in the evening, long after she'd given up hope. She was going to sing with a real live professional opera company.

It had started…

She embarrassed herself by shouting, 'I won,' and looked around wildly. But the worthy citizens of Edinburgh are quite blasé when it comes to people celebrating at all hours in their streets and, apart from a disapproving look from one middle-aged woman at the bus stop on the other side, no one appeared to be paying her the slightest attention.

Again she looked up at the building. How massive it was from here, a great circular building of stone. She walked up the steps to the front door. Of course, the door was locked, but she peered through the glass. She almost skipped back down the steps, touching the stonework as she went. She had heard of people hugging trees and now she felt like hugging a building. Isla laughed at herself. What long arms she would need to encircle this massive concert hall.

Time to go, to face a different kind of music. She had to break the news to everyone at home – her parents and Ross, her boss, probably the school district officer, too. Her excitement faded as the thought of her children, and the classroom where she and they had worked so hard and so creatively to-gether. Would they think she was abandoning them?

The homecoming was not nearly so bad as Isla had feared. Her mother was at Arbroath Station to meet the train. Isla spotted her from the carriage as she walked along, look-ing at the few people getting off, anxiously watching for her daughter. Her face cleared as she caught sight of Isla and, although not usually demonstrative in public, she hugged her daughter and kissed her cheek.

'We're that proud of you, Isla. Ross was on the phone this morning, and he's pleased for you too.'

They went quickly up the stairs, crossed the railway line and down the stairs on the other side. Isla thought her mum looked tired, as if she had not slept very well, and she grieved that she had inadvertently caused her pain.

'Oh, Isla love.' Mrs Wren shook her head when Isla challenged her. 'I meant what I said. Your dad and I are proud of you – we have always been proud of you. I didn't think anything could beat my feelings when I saw you get your degree...' Almost overcome with emotion, she swallowed once and went on. 'I just wish my mother had been alive to see you sing at the Usher Hall.'

They drove out to the small cottage where they lived on the Maxwell farm. Like the rest of the farm, it was neat and tidy. The windows shone with evidence of exuberant cleaning, and the brass knocker in the shape of a fox's head that was fixed to the front door had also been freshly polished. The little garden on either side of the paved pathway was neat and tidy, too. For most of the year it was alive with colour but now, at the beginning of winter, perennials had been cut back and only the berries of a holly bush in a corner and a few leggy, tired-looking chrysanthemums relieved the green.

Inside, though, all was colour, for Mrs Wren, a proud past-president of the local Women's Rural, was a talented embroiderer.

'It's good to be home.' Isla hung her coat on the hall stand. 'I love Edinburgh, and the flat's fabulous, Mum, but...'

Her mother nodded, understanding what an enormous step her young daughter had just taken. She guessed at the doubts and anxieties that were running through Isla's mind. 'I'll put the kettle on, and you can tell me every wee detail before your dad gets home. Furniture and curtains have about as much appeal for him as football has for me. You can tell me all about the audition too.'

The telephone rang when her mother was in the kitchen, and Isla jumped up to answer it.

'Hello, Isla.'

Why she had not expected it to be Ross, she had no idea. But her heart began to beat rapidly and her stomach to flip over, and she knew that she loved him. If he were to ask her again, would she stay?

'Ross, how are you?' She cringed at the words. What a stupid thing to say to a jilted fiancé.

'Come for a walk with me. We need to talk.'

She twisted the telephone cord around her fingers. The pain in her heart was fresher than ever. 'We talked and talked already.' She pushed her knuckles into her mouth to stop herself from sobbing.

'I'm not going to try to make you change your mind, but I need to see you. You owe me that much, Isla.'

She knew that was true.

They agreed to meet at the foot of the original school road that ran into a lane leading to the main farmhouse. There was a lilac tree and, farther along, a huge horse chestnut. How often they had met there – in spring to cut sprays of beautifully perfumed purple flowers, in autumn to collect chestnuts. For the past two years Ross had collected them for Isla's class.

Her heart thumped when she saw him. Ross had never seemed aware of his good looks, but by any standard he was a handsome young man. His eyes were beautiful, just like Holly's, but with the even longer lashes, something that had infuriated his sister and embarrassed him.

They did not speak, but automatically turned and walked together towards the opening to the school road.

'When do the rehearsals start?'

'Beginning of January.'

He nodded. 'Just like the school. Have you put in your notice yet?'

Isla explained that she had an appointment with her head teacher before school the next morning. 'She's been amazingly supportive. I mean...'

He filled the silence. 'I'm going up to the new farm tomorrow. Mum and Dad will come with me to help me settle in. I think I'll stay up there, a lot of work to do.'

'I'm sorry, Ross. So very, very sorry.'

'Don't be.' For once he did not sound like himself. 'I'm looking forward to the opportunity, Isla. My own farm, at my age – it's exciting. I'm going to run sheep, and it's almost time to put the rams with the ewes if I want early lambs for the shows.'

She smiled, aware of how much her father would love to have helped him.

'Your new life will be exciting, too,' he went on. 'I want you to be a professional singer – that is, if it's what you want. Those people in the opera company know better than me and everybody here. Go for it, Isla. I know I said some harsh things, but I've been thinking. What if we had married and there we were, up in Aberdeenshire on our farm, and you realised you would rather be at that La Scala place? What then?'

She said nothing. What could she say?

'I love you, Isla Wren, always have, always will. Boring old farmer me. If you ever need me, I'm there for you.'

They had reached the other end of the road. She looked up at Ross and gasped at the pain in her heart. What was she doing? What was she throwing away so casually?

No, not casually. If that were true it wouldn't be hurting so much. Isla hoped he could guess at the thoughts in her head, and understand.

He took her cold hands in his and blew on them, just as he had done when she was a little girl. 'I'll probably see you at Christmas.'

Her eyes showed her pain.

'Don't say anything. I want you to follow your dream. Who knows, maybe someday it'll coincide with mine. Just go, Isla. Turn and walk away.'

She closed her eyes to blink away the tears – and he was gone.

Isla was wrong in thinking that no one she knew had seen her yell in public outside The Usher Hall. Simon Ashford had been driving down Lothian Road and, since the traffic was denser than normal because of all the work going on at the concert hall, he had time to let his gaze drift slightly, spotting the little redhead who'd passed him as he'd left Jenny Grant's flat. She had seemed upset that day, but looked quite different at this moment, shouting aloud. He laughed at her expression when she clearly realised that she was behaving in a most unladylike fashion.

Jenny was in the dialysis ward when, later that day, Simon reached the hospital. She and a colleague were standing by the bed of one of the frailer patients, who was experiencing difficulty after his dialysis machine had been disconnected. It happened occasionally, especially with very frail patients, and was always a cause of concern. Simon stood ready to assist. He would not interfere.

'I'm here if you need me.' He said to the two nurses, and moved away.

If you need me. Simon grimaced at his words. Once Jenny had needed him, though not professionally.

He remembered the first time he had ever seen her. Still a student, he had been late for a ward tour. Knowing the consultant would be furious, he had raced along corridors in Dumfries's Crichton Hospital as if his life depended on it.

Jenny, then a student nurse, had been at the nurses' station when, out of breath, he had slid in.

'Don't worry, Doc,' she'd teased. 'I won't let him eat you.'

Where had that easy humour gone?

He pushed the memories away and went back to work. It was almost two hours later before he saw Jenny again. She looked exhausted but, as always, every hair was in place. She was at the foot of a bed where a woman who appeared to be asleep lay propped up on a mountain of pillows.

Simon stood quietly and watched as Jenny picked up the patient's notes. She spoke quietly to her patient and then, to his surprise, she began to clean the patient's teeth.

'I wouldn't let my worst enemy go through this,' Simon whispered as he approached her.

Jenny did not look at him but spoke sombrely. 'She's probably the bravest person I have ever met. I can't even conceive of the idea of being unable to do anything. She resents this state, but has to accept help. Nursing is a privilege, I told her. Her son is coming and she likes to be fresh.' She turned to look at him. 'She used to be so lovely, Simon. I saw a picture.'

'Lovely,' he agreed but Jenny did not know that he was not looking at the patient.

Jenny stroked the lady's hand. 'She's not going to last much longer. And her son will be with her.' She spoke so quietly that he was not sure that he had heard. 'As will I.'

'Good night, Nurse Jenny Grant,' he said gently, and left the room.

Jenny heard him go, and wished that she could call him back. For too long she had denied the feelings she had for Simon Ashford. Now, in a moment of weakness and exhaustion, they had rushed back. She allowed herself to see him as he was – a dedicated, hard-working and tender man.

Hugh Crawford was late meeting Holly, who had been sipping coffee for almost an hour in the trendy wine bar. When she saw him arrive, looking very dishy in uniform, she was prepared to forgive him anything.

Subduing such unprofessional thoughts, she focused instead on convincing him that he would find her prepared for anything, never mind how tumbledown the building. He ordered coffee and then Holly got straight to the point.

'I thought we might start with something

cold, Major,' she said in a businesslike way. 'Paper-thin, rare smoked venison with one of my secret sauces, followed by braised chicken on a bed of wild rice with seasonal vegetables and an apple-cream sauce. I like to use food in season.'

His face fell. 'Not Brussels sprouts. And please, call me Hugh.'

'Holly,' she said in turn, and then rushed on. 'No, the marrow family, probably, and leeks. Then, for pudding – *crêpes soufflées*. Classic, elegant, light enough for small appetites and hearty enough for...' she was going to say soldiers and then thought that might be misunderstood ... 'even very large ones.'

'I'm hungry already.' He smiled at her.

His eyes were amazing, Holly decided. Sometimes grey as the stones on the bed of a highland stream, sometimes blue as a spring sky. But this was business. 'Good,' she managed to say in response.

'The dining-room is miles from the kitchens, Holly,' he warned.

'I'll manage.' For some reason she found it difficult to call him Hugh.

'I have no doubt of that. By the way, I do have some staff at the castle. They'll do the clearing up and help with whatever you need.'

When they left the restaurant they found that the weather had changed and an early snow was falling.

'Where's your car?'

'I'll catch a bus; there are plenty of them.'

He looked up at the leaden sky. 'I'll drive you home.' With his hand under her elbow he guided her along the street. 'It won't settle,' he said as he opened the passenger door. 'Too early.'

Since she had no choice, Holly gave him directions and less than fifteen comfortable minutes later she was delivered to her flat.

Inside the flat Holly found Jenny already in her pyjamas, painting her toenails. 'Hugh drove me home.' At last she spoke his name.

'In a tank?' Jenny looked up from her toes

to the re-run she was watching on television.

'Very funny.' Holly flopped down beside her friend and glanced at the screen. 'What are you watching? This has got to be the fifth time that detective has solved that particular crime.'

Jenny surveyed her toes and got up. 'Nurses take what they can get, when they can get it. I'll heat up the casserole.'

They moved into the kitchen and Holly sat down at the table.

'Tell me all,' said Jenny, joining her.

'We talked about the menu.'

'And?'

'He approved it, so we said thank you to each other and went outside – it's snowing, did you know? – and before I could say, I'll see you on Sunday, or something equally banal, I was in his car and being driven home.'

'Masterful,' Jenny teased as she ladled a simple tuna macaroni bake on to the plates. 'I'd hate to be one of his junior men.'

'Actually, it was quite pleasant having someone decide for me ... and only an idiot would stand waiting for a bus when a perfectly nice car was available.'

'Do you fancy him?'

Holly grinned. 'Who wouldn't? There is something about a uniform, any kind of uniform, isn't there?' She looked at her friend sharply as she reached for the French bread. 'But I think of him as a client, sort of like a boss. The way you think of Simon Ashford.'

Jenny stood up to put on the kettle. 'I'll make some tea – and I never think of Simon Ashford.'

'Sit down, old chum.' Holly snatched at Jenny's pyjamas to stop her leaving. 'Let's agree not to discuss the men in our lives tonight. But we do need to get things straight about Isla before she moves in. She's so thrilled about this opportunity, though miserable about breaking up with Ross. I'm unhappy about it, too. Ross is my brother, and he's devastated. Mum's beside herself, and Dad is saying nothing, always a bad sign with him. I don't even want to think about Isla's parents.'

'Can you forgive her?'

Holly bent her head. 'I want to but I keep thinking, why on earth didn't she choose singing years ago? Then the engagement would never have taken place.'

'You don't know that, Holly. Ross and Isla have always had a special bond. Well work will take her mind off Ross, and in a few months she may reconsider – and Ross too. But there mustn't be tension in this flat, or all three of us will fall out, and that would be awful.' Jenny stood up again. 'I've had a long day, Hol, I'm off to bed.'

They said goodnight. As she finished her meal Holly went over her time with Hugh Crawford, and admitted to herself that she had enjoyed every moment, every word, every look.

She went to the sink to wash up, but instead of the dishes but she was seeing Jenny when they had spoken of Simon Ashford.

I wish I knew what he feels about Jenny,

she thought, for what she thinks about him is written all over her face.

'You do understand that I won't be coming back after the Christmas holidays?' Isla was facing her class of lively eight-year-olds.

'Oh, aye, Miss. It'll be great seeing you on the TV,' was one small boy's verdict.

His classmates hushed him and Isla smiled and remembered how fond she was of all of them. Her head teacher, the children, and, as far as she could see, the entire staff – even the rather grumpy janitor – were absolutely behind her. Each seemed to take her success as a personal triumph.

She was determined that the last few weeks of her teaching career would be memorable. Christmas preparations were always fun, but had to be fitted in to a busy curriculum. Isla made her plans, studied the music that would herald her new career, and tried not to notice how very heavy her heart was.

One cold, frosty evening, as she left the school, she found her father with his favourite dog by the gate.

'Carry your books, Miss?' he teased. 'I thought I'd maybe walk you home, lass. It's almost as bright as day with those stars and I was minding on how you aye liked to walk in the moonlight with me and old Jess here.'

Isla smiled and handed him her briefcase. She bent down as if to fondle the ears of the Border collie at her knees, but really to hide the tears which she could feel welling up in her eyes. How transparent her father was ... and how loving.

They turned together and walked along, for a moment just enjoying being together. Isla spoke first. 'Look, the moonlight is making a pathway across the river. Do you remember how I used to think that path would actually bear my weight?'

'Aye, and I remember thinking that in years to come I'd get to show the same moonpaths to your own wee ones.'

'You still can, Dad, just not yet.'

'And not here, eh? Do they have rivers in New York?'

Isla stopped walking. 'I've gone too far to back out now, Dad. And who knows, maybe I'll fail. There are thousands of people out there trying to make it.'

'You won't fail, lass. The idea of my wee Isla failing at anything she set her heart on has never occurred to me, or your mum.'

She looked up at him, tears again sparkling in her eyes, and wondered that her father had had to come out to view the wonders of nature, in order to say things to her that he couldn't utter while sitting by his own fireside. 'Thank you. I know you've always been a support, and I am going to give this opportunity all I've got. Sometimes I dream that there's a moonpath somewhere that will take me to the world's stage. But I'm being practical, Dad. I have six months with the company, and I'll need to find a good singing teacher to help me. There's so much I have to learn. But after the six months, who knows what will happen.'

'Was it hard to give Ross back his ring?'

She thought of the weeks of worrying.

'The hardest thing I've ever done in my life. I wish I could explain, Dad. I wish I really understood, myself. I love Ross, yet I hurt him. Why?'

'Maybe to be cruel to be kind. Ross is a nice laddie, but you'll likely meet other lads and he'll meet nice lassies. It seems a marriage at this particular time just isnae the right way for you – or the lad.'

She sighed with relief. Her father had been so thrilled when she'd become engaged to Ross, his employer's only son, a boy he'd known since the day he was born. 'I had to set him free.' She could say no more.

'Aye. I'm right proud that you love him enough to have done that.' He took her arm and they began to walk again. 'Come on. I'm freezing, and your mum will have the tea on. Can I ask what Holly's saying about it, Isla? Cannae be easy for her.'

'It isn't. She's been marvellous, but it's obvious she's being pulled two ways. She must be angry with me for hurting her brother, but we've been friends all our lives

92

and have always sworn to stand by one another. I've decided to stay in the flat at first, but if there's any tension, any anger, then I will leave. Maybe losing Holly and Jenny's friendship is another price I have to pay.'

'Nothing worthwhile comes easy,' her father commented, and they walked home.

Major Hugh Crawford's Keep was not an enormous castle, but rather a tall rectangular tower with smaller wings on either side. 'I could see an American film company loving this,' Holly said to herself as she pulled up in a cobblestone courtyard before imposing wooden doors. There was evidence of summer colour in the few plants that flourished against the walls but, so late in the year, the castle looked gaunt and mainly unwelcoming.

'Honeysuckle all over that wall and a bed of scented roses over there would make all the difference,' she decided as she began to unload.

An elderly woman showed her to kitchens that were vast and cold. 'We had a wee bit trouble with the boiler this morning, but everything's purring along nicely at the moment. Sir Hugh is with his factor the now but we can get started.'

Sir Hugh? That was unexpected. Major Hugh had been daunting enough.

The woman, who introduced herself as Mrs Bruce, showed Holly the kitchen, the pantries and a stone-walled room she called the scullery, where a state of the art dishwasher stood in splendid isolation. 'It's a wee walk from the dining room down to here, but this fair washes everything a treat. Except the crystal and the silverware,' she added. 'I do them in the old butler's pantry. There hasn't been a butler in it since World War One, but we like to keep up traditions here.'

When Mrs Bruce had gone, Holly looked around the antiquated kitchen and tried not to groan. Please let it all work, she said to herself silently. First, she checked the hot-plates, and was delighted to find that they were indeed hot. She had never seen ovens like these elderly ones, and once more breathed a prayer that the crêpes would be successful.

Wrapping a workmanlike apron around her small waist, she closed her eyes for a second, and began.

Hours later she heard Hugh Crawford's voice. 'I thought you might like some coffee – you've been labouring away for ages.'

He looked as he had the first time they had met – very Scottish country gentleman. 'Thank you,' she said.

He handed her a cup of coffee. 'It's quite a step to the dining room, but I don't expect you to wait at table. Everyone knows that you're on your own tonight. I'll manage myself, and Evelyn will be here, too.'

'Thank you,' she said again, sipping her coffee.

'It's a bachelor and soldier's house. Everything is planned for best success with least effort. Mrs Bruce has set the tray for coffee in the drawing room, so if you have it ready at the end of the meal I'll come for the pot. It's heavy.' He gestured over to the ornate, solid-silver coffee-pot on a sideboard, and spotted the tray that Holly had put there. He lifted the cloth. 'Mm, chocolate mousse.'

Holly flushed with embarrassment. 'Just in case the crêpes let me down.'

'What you mean is, in case my old ovens let you down. I almost hope they do. Chocolate mousse comes a close second to apple pie in my book.'

'You haven't tasted my chocolate mousse,' she teased.

He laughed. 'I'm off to meet the early guests, but I cannot resist a challenge and that, Miss Holly Maxwell, was a challenge.'

He walked off, and Holly laid out the perfectly cooked butternut squash, which set off the chicken breasts beautifully. She stood admiring it for a second, and was then interrupted by an elegantly dressed Evelyn and another, even more sophisticated, woman.

'How is it all going?'

Before Holly could answer Evelyn introduced the other woman, who was looking so
keenly at Holly as to make her slightly nervous. 'This is Samantha Gracie. Sam, what
do you think of my protégée?'

'I'll wait until I've had dinner to decide,'
Samantha replied coldly and moved as if to
lift the cloth on the tray.

Evelyn stalled her. 'You'll be delighted.
Hugh wouldn't have hired Holly just on my
say so. Come along, Sam, we're in the way.'
She looked round quickly. 'I'd put a huge
kettle on the hob now if I were you, Holly,'
she suggested. 'The electricity in this Keep
is a law unto itself, and you might just need
a back up.'

She escorted her friend to the door, and
popped her head in when Samantha Gracie
was out of earshot. 'I can't wait, Holly – it
will be marvellous. Don't worry about Sam.
Her late husband was Hugh's best friend,
and since he was killed in action she watches
over Hugh like a mother hen. He's the

person least like a helpless chicken that I know, but she likes to think of herself as family, and possibly it eases her own loneliness.'

'I'm sorry for her loss,' Holly said automatically. Even though she's a very unpleasant hen, she added in her thoughts as she carried on with her work

Time passed in a blur of activity. The electricity behaved itself, and after the pudding, the crêpes, had been served and eaten, Major Crawford came down for the coffee pot. 'Holly, that was fabulous. I do hope there is enough left for you?'

'Yes, thank you. Mrs Bruce has invited me to join her in her room.'

'Praise indeed.' He smiled. He set the coffee pot down and moved closer to her. 'Were you planning to rush back to Edinburgh? It's just that...'

Whatever he was about to say then was interrupted by Samantha. 'Good heavens, Hugh, darling, our guests are organising a search party.' She took his arm and turned to Holly. 'I take it you did manage to make coffee, then. We will have to do something about this kitchen, Hugh.'

Before Holly could speak Samantha spotted the waiting coffee-pot and turned her gaze on Hugh. 'Let's hope that's not gone cold. Come along, darling. You can chat with the hired help later.'

Episode 4

Christmas was not the joyful family occasion it had always been. Holly stayed in Edinburgh since Fabulous Foods was extremely busy, and Evelyn needed her. Isla was aware that, if she went home as she longed to do, she would be bound to meet Ross or his parents, so she took a trip to London on the pretence of doing research for her first role.

Only when she was sitting in a darkened theatre, with wonderful music all around her, did it hit her that, for the first time in her life, she was not at home for Christmas and that her mother and father, too, would be alone.

So only Jenny went home to the village. As always, the Grants worked long and hard in the shop on Christmas Eve. There was always someone who had forgotten to buy at least one ingredient for the Christmas meal, or who needed a gift for a last-minute guest. Jenny put on an apron and helped out.

'Just like the old days, love,' her father said with a smile as they arranged 'special offers' on a table.

With Jenny to help in the shop, her mother spent most of the morning next door in their little cottage. But in the late afternoon she brought through some freshly baked biscuits. 'Come away into the back, Jenny, and we'll make some tea. Your dad'll shout if he needs you.'

Jenny and her father exchanged a knowing

look. Clearly her mother wanted to talk, though she waited till they were seated at the table, piled high with unsold calendars and Annuals which would be reduced the following week.

'Lovely biscuits, Mum, Jenny enthused.'

'Good. Now, love, it's none of my business, but we're all a bit worried about you three. The Maxwells say Holly hardly tells them a thing.' She looked at her daughter shrewdly. 'No secrets, lass, but is she seeing this soldier? He's a bittie older, surely, being a Major.'

Jenny looked into her cup evasively. 'I know she has business dealings with him,' she said at last. 'Anything else, you'll have to ask Holly.'

Her mum got up and refilled their cups. 'Here, take a cup to your dad.' She sounded quite cross.

'I know it's none of my business,' she began again when Jenny returned, 'but is Simon Ashford still at the Infirmary? Sorry, it's just your dad and I always liked him,

Jenny. We never learned what happened between you two, and now, him turning up at the same hospital just seems...'

'Don't go there, Mum,' Jenny warned as she stood up. 'Simon broke my heart once and once is enough.'

To soften the rebuke, she kissed her mother gently as she passed her and returned to the shop, leaving the older woman looking sadly at her daughter's unfinished cup of tea.

For as long as she could remember, Jenny had visited the parents of her two friends on Christmas Eve and later, carrying parcels, she continued the tradition. The village was like a picture on a Christmas card. The great stone church stood on its own, light flooding from the stained-glass windows and sending streams of colour over the white-frosted grass in the churchyard, where the huge holly bush near the wall offered its red berries to hungry wintering birds. Each cottage boasted rows of lights along the eaves and a decorated tree in every living-room and excited children ran from one house to the next and back again, delirious with expectation.

Jenny left the village and drove up to the Maxwell farm, where she was pleased to find that Holly's parents and Isla's were spending the evening together. They talked – avoiding, Jenny thought, the subjects foremost in their minds – and they laughed. Everyone was going through the motions, doing what they had always done – the Watchnight service, the gifts and the lovingly prepared meals. But they were all glad when the holidays were over.

Although Holly had been downcast, having put certain hopes to rest concerning Major Hugh Crawford, over the Christmas period she had enjoyed working so hard. She now felt a complete professional, one able to put business before her private life. Lunches, dinners, even children's parties, Evelyn was catering them all and Holly threw herself into doing perfect work.

The children's parties were best, as there

was no chance there of bumping into Hugh. Sir Hugh, she reminded herself, and out of your league as merely "the hired help." The catty words of Samantha Gracie still rankled.

She had waited for him to make personal contact after the dinner she had catered for him, but there had only been a cheque with a brief note of thanks. Mind you, the note did say that the food had been perfect and that all his guests had begged for her telephone number. 'Especially Samantha, I'm sure,' Holly had remarked sourly to herself as she folded the note and put it away in a drawer.

Once, she thought she spotted Hugh at one of the evening parties, but since she'd spent the evening in the kitchen she could not be sure. When Evelyn came in to check on things she'd spoken to her, striving to sound casual. 'Evelyn, is Major Crawford here tonight?'

'Hugh? No, I haven't seen him since before Christmas. Sometimes he disappears without warning. It's the nature of his job.' She looked at Holly measuringly. 'I'm glad I didn't fall in love with a soldier; I couldn't stand the strain.'

Holly felt herself blushing at her employer's words. In love? She turned away.

'Sometimes he has early warning of an assignment, so he alerts his close friends. Other times, though, he just goes and then, one day he's back.'

'It must be frustrating for Samantha.'

Evelyn turned in surprise. 'Samantha? She does tend to mother Hugh – or try to, as I told you. But truth to tell, he's never really liked her, Holly. Her husband was his closest friend but there's no more to their relationship than that.'

Holly busied herself with her dishes, certain the crimson on her cheeks could now rival the lights on Evelyn's Christmas tree. Her heart was behaving in a decidedly erratic way. She was scarcely aware of Evelyn patting her comfortingly on the shoulder before returning to the party.

At holiday periods the hospital was always busier than ever, but Jenny shone when dealing with added strain. She noticed that Simon was not on duty, but she said nothing. If Simon Ashford decided to take a holiday over the Christmas and New Year period, well, that was none of her business.

'Doctor Ashford wasn't down on the rota to have Christmas leave,' Staff Nurse O'Donnell speculated as she fiddled with a length of tinsel. 'Bit odd, don't you think?'

'Who knows? Maybe he got a great deal on a skiing holiday and jumped at the chance.'

'Maybe he got hit by a bus.'

'Then he'd be here, and we'd all know.' She would not think about Simon. It would be a relief not to have him around for a while, to give her a chance to get her mind straight. Half of her hoped that he had transferred to another hospital, while the other half acknowledged that life would be almost unbearable if she could no longer see

106

him every day. It was like toothache, she decided. The more you poked the sore spot with your tongue, the more it hurt

She went into the city when her shift was over with the intention of looking at the after-Christmas sales (which had been running since before Christmas). Princes Street, with gardens, art galleries and monuments on one side and its private clubs, shops and small cafés on the other, was blocked to traffic because of road works.

She sighed, annoyed to find herself on the gardens side of the road and with no immediate idea of how to get across to where Jenners, the world-renowned department store, stood.

She launched herself forward ... almost into the path of an earth-mover. There was a grinding of gears, and a muffled oath from the driver, and Jenny found herself with legs shaking so much that she could scarcely stand. The understandably annoyed driver climbed down from his cab and advanced on her, his face white with shock.

Then a strong, familiar arm went round her shoulders. 'Let me help. I'm a doctor.' Jenny found herself being led to the pavement. 'I'll attend to her.'

'All right then.' The driver scowled. 'What a fright she gave me.'

Simon hurried Jenny along the pavement, and a few minutes later they had managed to lose themselves in the crowd crossing at traffic lights further along. His arm was still around her as they entered Jenners. 'A cup of tea will set you to rights. What on earth possessed you to throw yourself in front of that thing?'

'I thought the way was clear; I misjudged it, that's all,' she retorted, dislodging his arm.

'Misjudgement. That's not like you, Jenny. Think of the poor man – you've aged him ten years.'

Of all the people to come to her rescue, she thought, as he found them a table.

'I do not need tea.'

'But I do. Seeing someone you care for

attempt to immolate herself as a protest against road improvements is very stressful.'

Jenny sat back in her chair and took a breath. Had Simon really said he cared about her, or was he merely trying to be clever or funny?

'Two teas, please,' he said to the hovering waitress. 'And chocolate cake, I think. That always was a favourite of yours, Jenny, wasn't it?'

She nodded weakly. 'We haven't seen you for a week or two in the wards.'

'Did you miss me?' Though the question could have been flippant, Simon's face was serious, his eyes questioning.

Had Jenny missed him? Only every minute of every day.

As the waitress arrived with their order she tried to remember when they had last sat together here drinking tea and eating cake. He had remembered that she loved chocolate. What else did he remember? 'Did you have a nice Christmas?'

'I went home, Jenny. My brother was

injured in a road accident a few days before Christmas.'

Impulsively she reached across the little table and took his hand. 'Simon, how awful. Your poor mum – and brother of course.'

'He's improving, and Mum's bearing up.' His face was drawn and tired. He leaned back a little and tried to smile. 'It's been a long time since we've had tea together here.'

'There was a tablecloth on that table over there; pristine white, and with creases that could have cut butter.'

'The cake was not so good though.'

'We had scones.'

They smiled at each other, rediscovering the ease of earlier days. 'We sound like something from an old film,' Simon said. 'And yes, I do remember it well.' He squeezed her hand. 'I've missed you so much, Jenny.'

Something in her heart relaxed as she recognised that now, at last, it was time to talk. There was silence for a moment though, as they sat, just looking at each other.

It was Jenny who broke the spell. 'Have we both grown up in the last five years?'

He had no time to answer for another voice interrupted. 'Simon, darling, where ever have you been?'

Startled, they looked up.

A beautiful, sophisticated young woman wearing a full-length suede coat stood there smiling at Simon, her arms outstretched. He got to his feet and returned the woman's embrace.

'Good Lord, is that the time?' Jenny stood up more slowly, looking at her watch as if she had just remembered something. 'Must go, sorry.'

And she walked as quickly as she could from the restaurant.

'I can't believe how stupid I was, Holly.'

Back at the flat she had found her friend curled up on the sofa. 'First, I nearly fall in front of an earth-mover. Then, just as we begin to talk – really talk, Hol, like we used to do – this glamour model turns up, wearing a coat that probably cost at least half a year's salary and practically throws herself into Simon's arms.'

'In Jenners of all places? Shock, horror.' Holly patted her friend ineffectually. 'Come on, Jenny, think. Simon's successful, good-looking and unattached. He's bound to have friends, and among those there must be women who find him attractive. But remember, he was having tea with you.'

'And I ran away like a silly little girl.' Jenny sat down on the sofa and buried her face in her hands.

Holly hugged her. 'You did very well in the circumstances.'

'I feel so stupid. What must he think?'

Holly suspected several things that Dr Simon Ashford might be thinking but kept her own counsel. 'All I know is that you must not let it drop like this. Jenny, he still likes you. Talk to him tomorrow. Say you wish you could have finished your cake – anything – but don't let it stop there.'

Jenny got to her feet. 'I feel an absolute

fool. I'm going to bed.'

She tossed and turned all night, and in the morning felt no better.

When Isla returned from London she moved into the tiny room that Holly and Jenny had prepared for her. The situation was fraught with difficulty. Could Holly disregard the fact that she was sharing her home with the girl who had jilted her beloved brother?

She was determined to make it work, however, and on Isla's first evening with them she prepared a special dinner. All three worked hard, possibly too hard, at conversation, but eventually they relaxed, and their chatter as they drank coffee was easier.

'I've put my name down as a supply teacher,' Isla told them. 'There are so many schools in Edinburgh that, surely, I'll find work. Two or three days a week would be ideal.'

Jenny and Holly looked at each other and

then at their friend. 'Teaching?' They asked together.

'I need to pay my way. This is a semi-professional opera company, not Covent Garden. My salary is laughable so substitute teaching would at least be an income of some kind. I couldn't take a long-term post. The performances will be in the evenings but some rehearsals must take place during the day, as well.'

'You'd have a better chance with the private schools if you're teaching music, I would imagine,' Jenny speculated.

'Actually I've requested music or primary teaching. I can't remember ever having a substitute music teacher when we were in primary, though. Can you?'

The girls thought for a while.

'Once a week we had that funny wee man with bad breath,' Holly offered.

'And weren't we thrilled when he didn't turn up. Who knows, maybe his halitosis was what encouraged me into nursing,' Jenny chipped in.

Soon all three were laughing just as they had done all through school and university. Isla went to bed that night in her tiny bedroom, reflecting on how very lucky she was. The next hurdle was to find out if the reality of life as a singer would in any way be as wonderful as the dream.

Instead of 'Carmen', his first choice of opera, the producer had chosen to do Mozart's 'The Marriage of Figaro'. At first Isla had been afraid that her part, that of Susanna, the Countess's maid, would be too demanding, but she had studied it and was now quite sure that her acting talent was up to its exacting standard. She would not allow herself to worry about her voice. The judging panel had obviously thought it capable of handling the challenges of her solos, as well as the duets she would have to sing with the two male leads, both professional singers.

Isla walked up to the first company meeting with her fingers firmly crossed inside her mittens. Her heart was heavy because, more than anything, she found herself wishing that Ross were there to encourage her.

The first rehearsal was only a little more stressful than those she had had at college. The company met in a cold and gloomy church hall in Morningside, an added bonus, as Isla could walk to and from rehearsals. The only new member of the company, she was introduced to a seemingly enormous group of people. How on earth would she remember names and what they did? There was a producer, rehearsal pianist, director, conductor, stage manager and countless others, each with an assistant.

Apologies were read out from the leading soprano, who was working abroad, as from the famous baritone, Hugo Williams, who was singing in the role of Figaro in Cardiff. Isla had been looking forward nervously to singing with the great man and hardly knew whether to be glad or sorry that she would have to wait another month.

Yet again, she realised that it was at times like this that it had always been reassuring to talk to Ross about all her new experinces.

The 'books' without which no perform-ance can possibly succeed were laid out on a table. The director took her through them.

'Wardrobe book. Everything you're going to wear is sketched in this book – and how to care for it. Stage-management book – each cue has been worked out and is here. These cues will not change.' He opened the third book, 'And this is the Production Move book. We've spent weeks working out every basic move; these, too, will not change. Learn them.' He looked at Isla and his rather stern face softened. 'Good idea to know where everyone else is supposed to be.'

Then there were warm-up exercises, accompanied by the usual poor jokes about warming up the hall first.

'Sorry,' Stephan Lenton, the conductor, confessed. 'My fault. I was an hour late put-ting the heat on; traffic problems.'

'The new tramway system will provide perfect alibis for months.' A cynical voice came from the back of the group.

'No, no. Tonight was a one off. Ready, and...'

At nine there was a short break and schedules were handed out for rehearsals. Sometimes the conductor would be working with the chorus only, and so there would be no need for principals to attend. At other times he would concentrate on individuals. These complicated schedules had taken a great deal of thought, and Isla discovered with a shock that, although she had the lesser of the soprano roles, she was also expected to understudy the lead role, just in case.

'Sorry, Isla, but you're easier – and cheaper – to replace as Susanna.'

The conductor smiled, which made him look less stern. Isla decided that he had no doubt forgotten that they had worked together once before. It had been her second year in college, and she had sung in the college choir for a performance of Handel's 'Messiah'.

'You'll be fine,' he said now. 'You were

always a bright student.'

He smiled even more widely, as if he could read her mind, and walked off to speak to the producer, Aldo Angelosanto, who was on leave from a professional Italian company.

Isla hugged herself mentally. Stephan Lenton had remembered her.

She told Jenny all about the rehearsal when she reached the flat just after eleven.

'Fantastic. You're barely started, and already an up-and-coming conductor is interested in you. I think I'd sit down and learn everybody's parts, if I were you.'

'I'd say we all end up doing that. Can't help absorbing what we hear all day.'

'Spoken like a true professional.'

Leaving Isla, Jenny went off to make some cocoa.

The following evening Jenny arrived home just as the telephone rang. Being closest, she picked up the receiver. When she heard the voice on the other end she blushed furiously, was quiet for a moment and then mumbled,

'No, I'm not doing anything important.'

Tactfully, Isla and Holly hurried past her and closeted themselves in the kitchen.

Jenny smiled as they passed, and then turned back to the call. 'I haven't been avoiding you, Simon. There was an emergency admission.'

Her heart raced. Since their unsatisfactory meeting, with its abrupt ending, she had not sought him out at the hospital. Now it was he who had made contact.

'I'm sitting in my car outside your flat, and I see there's a very pleasant little restaurant within walking distance. Don't tell me you've eaten already – you can't have had time. Please, Jenny. Our last personal conversation was, what shall we say, sabotaged?'

A few minutes later her flatmates heard the door close, then the sound of Jenny's heels as she ran down the stone stairs.

'I think that means that it's just two for dinner.' Holly raised an eyebrow at Isla.

Outside, Jenny saw Simon standing under

the street light. Without a moment's hesitation she ran across to him and was enfolded in his arms.

'Oh, Jenny, my beautiful, beautiful Jenny. What a fool I've been.'

She could say nothing and there, under the light, oblivious of anyone passing, they kissed. All the pent-up emotions of years burst forth and they spoke at the same time, neither able to understand a word the other said. Then he held her away from him, looking at her as if he would never tire of seeing her in his arms.

She stared back, shaking her head slowly. 'You ignored me for so long, Simon. I never understood why.'

'I thought it was for the best. You seemed set on gaining more and more qualifications, furthering your career. Then your father told me he hoped you intended to go to medical school. And you often used to talk about working abroad.'

'There's valuable work to do be done here.'

'I know. I should never have let your dad's

words sway me, Jenny. But I decided I should step out of the picture, give you space. I can't tell you how wonderful it was to see you again, here in Edinburgh. Why didn't you become a medical student?'

'That was Dad's dream, Simon, not mine. He's accepted now, that I've never wanted to do anything other than be a nurse. Besides, you must agree that renal medicine is so fulfilling – exciting even.'

He looked down into her eyes and laughed. 'That's my Jenny.' He kissed her nose. 'Cold. Have you noticed that it's snowing?'

Surprised, Jenny looked up to see the snow drifting down gently through the light, almost as a benediction...

Alone together for the first time since the engagement had been broken, Isla and Holly were a little nervous at being left. Holly busied herself ironing while Isla studied the musical score. Apart from a few remarks about their hopes for Jenny they were quiet, each lost in her own thoughts,

It was Holly who broke the silence. 'We really have made a mess of our private lives, haven't we? Or our love lives, that is.'

'Do you hate me, Holly?'

'Hate you? No. Why should I? You've been my friend all my life. No. Ross doesn't hate you, nor do our parents.'

'I do love him, you know.'

'Breaking off your engagement is a funny way of showing it.' Holly spoke without thinking.

Isla stared at her, aghast, then burst into tears and ran from the room. Holly heard the bedroom door slam, then she sat down in a chair by the table and put her head in her hands, furious with herself.

She had been tired lately, she knew, working too hard. She had thought the extra effort worthwhile. For one thing, the experience would be excellent, and for another the extra money would come in very useful for the flat. An additional plus was that there would be no time left over to think about anything ... or anyone. Holly had realised, from the moment that Evelyn had spoken about Hugh in the kitchen, that she was indeed falling in love with someone she hardly knew.

But at present she could do nothing. If Major Crawford cared for her he would contact her, and meantime she would wait.

She stood up. 'OK, Holly,' she said out loud. 'You need to put this right.'

She spent the next hour doing what she did best. Then, aware that the flat was full of mouth-watering smells, she went to Isla's door and knocked. 'Isla, I'm sorry, I didn't mean what I said, and I should never have said it at all. Come and have supper with me, or at least let me bring you a tray. Please.'

Just when she had decided that Isla had either fallen asleep or was too angry with her to respond, the door opened and Isla, in her dressing gown, appeared.

'I really am so sorry, Isla. It was harsh of me.'

'No. You were right, Holly. But I thought I

was doing the right thing – for both of us – at the time.'

They hugged and, arm in arm, walked back to the kitchen. Holly had set the table with her brightest, most cheerful, everyday dishes, and a large rustic casserole sat on a mat in the centre of the table. A crisp green salad and some lovely warm bread completed the picture.

There was silence for a while as both hungry girls enjoyed the delicious meal. Then, the same subject uppermost in both their minds, they spoke together.

'Wonder what Jenny's eating right now?'

'Bet Jenny won't taste a thing tonight.'

They laughed. 'Wouldn't you think that a really beautiful girl like Jenny would have no problems in the love department?'

'I know. Intelligent too.'

'I suspect that sometimes it's her intellect that gets in the way. You know how our Jenny always likes to analyses everything.'

'Look who's talking.' Isla began, just as they heard Jenny's returning footsteps on the stairs. They began to clear the table when they heard Jenny open the door quietly and slip into the hall. Once they were sure that she was alone, they went out to greet her.

'Had a good time?' Isla asked innocently.

'What about the food?' Holly chimed. 'There's lots here, still warm if you were too besotted to eat.'

'Very funny. Goodnight, girls. I'm up early in the morning.'

'No, you don't. Tell us everything.' Holly grabbed a laughing Jenny by her coat.

'OK. I'll tell you. We had lasagne, salad, ciabatti and a bottle of Chianti, followed by really excellent coffee. Bags I the bathroom first.'

Caught off guard, her friends could only stare as Jenny ran past them and into the flat's only bathroom.

Her heart lightened by Jenny's growing romance with Simon, Holly doggedly set her mind to learning as much as she possibly could from Evelyn and the others on the staff. As soon as her children had returned to school, Evelyn had gone off to France on a skiing trip, leaving her staff to carry on without her. It was a huge responsibility, and Holly wanted desperately to play her part well.

Up till now she had thought herself very well qualified, but theses days she was both humbled and amazed by the amount she was learning. A genius with sugar craft, Boris tried to encourage Holly to work with him.

'I think everything you do is amazingly beautiful, Boris. But you're an artist. I'm not.'

They were sitting at a small table in Evelyn's own kitchen that was set aside for staff members. Between them sat a bowl of monkfish pieces that had been roasted in a hot oven with cherry tomatoes, wine, fresh basil and garlic. 'You made this,' he pointed out. 'Is a work of art.'

'I'm not in your league, Boris, though. I think I'm scared of the heat of the sugar, and also, I'm sorry, but I'm not really interested in pretty desserts.'

'So we make the great team, no? You are a great chef. I am the best pastry cook and my spun sugar...'

He kissed his fingers, then laid his warm hand over hers, an amorous look in his big brown eyes. Holly thought quickly. She liked Boris and was happy to learn from him, but she had no wish to encourage him. Gently she disengaged her hand. 'Boris...'

'No, let me speak, Holly. I am watching you since the first day. Mrs Hammond says you will go out one day on your own. That's my dream, me. I could be your partner, maybe. What you say?'

'Thank you, I...'

He jumped up and kissed her. 'So you agree. We be partners.'

'No, Boris. I'm not ready to be partners with anyone. Please sit down here and finish your lunch.' She waited until he had settled himself and was sitting looking gloomily at his plate. 'I'm honoured that you would ask me, Boris, because I think you are an incredibly talented chef,' she started, trying to find words that would please without giving immediate hope. 'But I'm not ready to leave Fabulous Foods and, even if I were, I couldn't steal you away from Mrs Hammond. That wouldn't be ethical.'

Boris picked up his fork and speared a cube of the delicious fish. 'What is ethical? I don't know this word?'

'It means what is right.'

He thought for a moment. 'You have a boyfriend?'

Her mouth full, she merely shook her head.

'How about me, then?'

Holly stood up. She had to start the afternoon's work or they would be late and, more than anything she did not want to continue this conversation. 'No, Boris. I'm sorry, but no.'

'Then I better give you this letter.'

'Letter? What letter?' Holly watched him as he fished a very grubby and wrinkled envelope from his pocket.

'Mrs Hammond give me this on the Hogmanay and, I tell the truth, Holly, I forget it. Then she goes away and I think, maybe I don't need to give you.'

Trembling, Holly held out her hand. The stamped envelope was addressed to *Miss Holly Maxwell, C/o Mrs Evelyn Hammond.* On the bottom left was written clearly, *Please Forward.*

'Is from the soldier with the castle, Mrs Hammond say. You like the soldier with the castle, Holly? I'm sorry. Is the truth I forget. The Hogmanay and the party.'

Holly took the crumpled envelope and smiled at him. 'I know, Boris, and thank you for remembering.' She sat down and opened the envelope, which contained one sheet of good quality white notepaper. The letter was handwritten.

Dear Holly,
I am going away for a few months. That's the army for you.

May I write to you? E-mail me at the above address if the answer is yes.
Hugh

Holly wanted to dance. 'Boris,' she said instead, 'I have to go to the office for a moment. I'll be right back.'

As Holly's heart beat wildly and a thousand trapped butterflies cavorted around in her stomach, she raced upstairs to the catering office, knocked sharply and went in. Evelyn's secretary was stapling papers and looked up, in surprise.

'Michelle, this is an emergency and I'll square it with Evelyn but may I send one short e-mail from the office computer?'

'Go ahead. Is your family all right?'

'It's not that type of emergency.'

'Oh, the other kind of emergency, then – the man kind.' Michelle laughed and continued with her stapling and filing.

Holly tried to smile, but was too nervous. What if she were too late? What if he were no longer there? She sat down before the large desk-top machine and clenched and unclenched her fists several times before she began to type.

Hi, I'll look forward to hearing from you.

She signed it simply *Holly*, and, just in time, remembered to write her own email address before she pressed the *Send* button. She thanked Michelle and left the office, her mind in a whirl and her heart pounding in her chest. Hugh wanted to be in touch with her.

Boris drove Holly home in Evelyn's van. As she thanked him and got out, he looked at her sadly. 'You got time to change your mind,' he suggested.

She longed to rush upstairs to check e-mails, but she halted and turned to him. 'Boris, you're a great chef, and we work well together. But that's it.' She smiled. 'Goodnight.'

'Goodnight, Holly. See you tomorrow.'

As she opened the street door Holly heard him call after her, 'You still got time.'

She smiled and ran upstairs.

The flat was in darkness, apart from the little light the girls left in the hall for the last one arriving home. She took off her shoes, so as to be quiet on the wooden floors, and crept into her bedroom. Without taking off her coat she started up her laptop and waited.

There was only one e-mail. It was from her father about a cattle sale in Aberdeen.

In her bedroom, Isla lay listening. She heard Holly creep along to her bedroom and then go to the bathroom and wash. When her friend had slipped quietly back to bed, Isla got out of her own bed and turned on her bedside lamp. Since her long talk with Holly she had been thinking about what Ross's sister had said. *Breaking off your engagement is a funny way of showing you love Ross.*

'You're right, Holly,' she whispered. She sat down at her little table, picked up her pen, and began to write.

Episode 5

The wind shrieked around the roof tops of Edinburgh as if it were trying to collect chimney pots to send them crashing to the ground, but inside their flat, Holly, Jenny and Isla were warm and comfortable.

It was unusual for all three young women to spend an evening at home together. As a rule, Holly worked three or four evenings every week, and Isla had at least two evening rehearsals. Jenny, who worked a daytime shift at the hospital, spent more time alone in the evenings than did the others, but lately she, too, had found herself with evening plans that did not include her flatmates.

Tonight, she was curled up on the sofa reading a magazine and half-heartedly listening to the television programme her friends were watching. The programme was

134

interrupted by the loud ringing of a telephone, and suddenly all three girls were reaching for their own mobiles.

'It's the house 'phone,' Holly called as she almost ran into the hall.

Jenny and Isla sat, alert, but eventually a downcast Holly came back into the living room.

'Just a cold caller offering us cheaper broadband...'

Only Jenny heard the rest of the sentence, for a phone rang again, this time Isla's mobile.

'Hello?' she said, and then Jenny and Holly saw her blush becomingly and hurry from the room.

'Well, well,' Jenny said. 'She blushed, Hol. Do you think it was Ross?'

Holly, who had been hoping to hear from Hugh Crawford, tried to sound nonchalant. 'No idea. Either she'll tell us or she won't.'

In her bedroom, Isla was sitting on her bed, the receiver held to her ear and her heart pounding so loudly that she was sure it was audible. She was speaking, not to Ross, but to the musical director, Stephan Lenton. 'This Saturday? Yes, I'm free. It's awfully good of you.'

'Not at all, Isla. I'm sorry that it's such short notice. Your voice is perfect for the two solos. In fact, if I'd known you were available I would have asked you before.'

'But I have sung so little professionally.'

She heard him laugh. 'When I conducted my first concert, would you believe it, Isla, I hadn't conducted professionally at all. That's where we all start, at the bottom.'

Isla could hardly believe her ears. A famous Scottish soprano had come down with a virus, forcing her to cancel an engagement. Stephan Lenton was now asking Isla to fill in at the last minute – because he thought she was good enough. How many singers dream of such a moment, she wondered. The telephone rings, and suddenly a door to a magical world opens.

Had Isla the courage to walk into that world?

'Is that acceptable, Isla?'

She jerked out of her euphoria. She had been so overcome that she had barely heard the fee he had offered. 'It's wonderful, Stephan.'

'It's union rules,' he replied simply.

'What time is the rehearsal?' she asked, hoping she hadn't sounded too star-struck.

He became more business-like. 'When did you last sing those arias?'

'In college, with an amateur company.'

He laughed. 'Thought so. Right, dress rehearsal with the choir and orchestra on Saturday afternoon. Performance the same evening, in the Queen's Hall. If you're not teaching or whatever tomorrow you had better come over to my flat and work with me. We'll have a sandwich and make a day of it. Does that suit?'

She wanted to shout out with excitement but managed to control her emotions. 'Of course.'

He gave her directions to his flat, and once the call was ended she lay back on her bed, going over and over the conversation. She was going to sing, as the featured soprano soloist at Edinburgh's lovely Queen's Hall. It was happening, it was actually happening ... and earlier than she had dared hope.

Then she groaned, and sat up. In her letter to Ross she had promised to visit on Saturday. If only Stephan had telephoned earlier. What on earth was she going to do? How would she explain it to Ross?

Of the three flatmates, only Jenny had not anticipated a telephone call that evening. She knew that Simon was on call, and would not ring her to chat. They had spoken to each other several times during the day and, standing side by side at the nurses' station, had managed to drink a quick cup of coffee while arranging their next private meeting. By now, her parents, her two best friends and Simon's mother all knew that she and Simon were now officially "an item" once again, but as yet the young couple had told none of their colleagues. They wanted to enjoy their new relationship, to build on their old one and to prepare for a future together.

In the hospital they would act as they had always done, with complete professionalism. But occasionally their hands would touch for a moment, their eyes would meet, and their joy would shine out for anyone to see. Most of Jenny's colleagues were sensitive, however, and only one had teased her about her obvious happiness.

'I see you managed to have coffee with a certain consultant without spilling it all over him.'

And, with a smile, Jenny had answered, 'Now why would I do that?' which told Nurse O'Donnell absolutely nothing.

Now, her heart singing, Jenny went off to check her wards. There had been an emergency admission, and she went to meet her new patient, a young mother with two small children. Mrs Macleod lay asleep as Jenny familiarised herself with her notes.

'Say a prayer for her, darling,' a soft voice said behind her. 'There is a slight possibility of a transplant. I'll know any minute now.'

She did not turn. 'I am praying. Oh, Simon, she is so young.'

'Yes, and we'll do everything we can for her. We sent her husband home to be with the children. She's a fighter, Jenny. She'll fight as hard as she can to stay with them, and we'll be with her every step of the way.'

She felt him move closer. 'I love you, Nurse Grant. See you later.'

She heard him moving off down the ward. For a few minutes more she stayed watching her new patient, and then she moved on.

Holly had checked her e-mails before going to bed and, although she knew there were no messages on her mobile phone, nevertheless she checked it again. Nothing.

Grow up, she scolded herself. Hugh was a professional soldier, with no free time for casual e-mails to hardly known women. She turned her face into the pillow, trying to drive Hugh Crawford's face from her mind. Finally, she fell asleep, determined that she would think of nothing but her work.

She woke early the next morning and washed and dressed, deliberately ignoring her computer. Eventually, however, she gave in, sat down on her bed, and opened up the laptop.

There was one email waiting for her.

Hello, lovely to hear from you. Rather busy, but have meetings in the house on the hill next week. Could we meet for a late supper?
  Hugh.

The house on the hill? Where on earth...? Then Holly laughed. Edinburgh Castle, of course. Was this an example of military code? How to reply? She didn't want to be too eager.

Hello, supper sounds wonderful. Where?
  Holly.

She turned off her machine, picked up her coat, bag and fleecy gloves and hurried out, grateful that her flatmates were not around, as she was too flustered to speak She walked to the New Town and picked up croissants, then, pink from exertion and cold but composed, Holly arrived at Fabulous Foods. Boris was already in the kitchen, and the smell of percolating coffee filled the large room.

'You walked, then?' He poured her a mug of coffee. 'You don't spend enough time on your poor feet?'

Holly hung up her coat and took the coffee from him with thanks. 'I love to walk on a cold, crisp day like today, Boris. You should try it.'

He shrugged. 'I spend years walking in the cold, Holly, and running. Me, I like the nice warm bus. What do you make today?'

Before she could answer, Evelyn Hammond, followed by the third chef, Lizzie Monroe, joined them. Evelyn ran through the day's tasks.

'Holly will be creating something exciting with salmon or with venison, which I'll try out on friends this evening, Boris. We have an enormous wedding booked at Easter. The bridegroom is American and his fiancée wants an authentically Scottish meal.'

All competent professionals, the chefs got to work and the morning sped past. Later in the morning, Evelyn returned to measure progress. When she was chatting with Holly about the sauce she planned to accompany the venison, Holly asked if there were any late nights booked for the following week.

Evelyn smiled. 'A date, Holly, perhaps? Not with Boris, I trust.'

'Hugh, actually?'

'But he's away, in... Oh, Holly, this is so typical. I love Hugh dearly, always have done. But soldiers, well, when they're being soldiers it seems to me that the Army is all they can think about. We poor women are supposed to wait around, and then jump when they deign to call. Regina got totally...' She stopped as she saw the expression on Holly's face. 'Oh, dear, you don't know about Regina.'

Possibly to hide her embarrassment, Evelyn bent over to help herself to a spoon of the paté. 'This is scrumptious. Let's all have it on toast for lunch.' She went to the door, stopped, and then turned self-consciously. 'Actually, I have so much work to get through. Holly, would you mind bringing some up to my office instead?' She smiled and mouthed, 'Give us a chance to talk.'

The chefs returned to their work stations and Holly forced herself to concentrate, although thoughts kept intruding. So there had been a Regina. So what? There had been other men in Holly's life, too. 'But none of them made me feel like this,' she muttered.

While she was preparing a tray for Evelyn, Boris handed Holly a plate on which he had set a heart, spun from sugar. It was exquisite. 'For you, Holly, queen of my heart.'

The heart was beautiful, but Holly wanted neither it, nor the underlying message Boris seemed to be sending with it. Was he serious? She hoped not. 'I'll give it to Evelyn, Boris.

She'll love it.'

She moved away, and thus did not see the expression of anger that crossed the pastry chef's face as she rejected his offering.

Isla found Stephan Lenton's beautiful flat quite easily. Part of a rather grand house in the Old Town near the castle, its magnificent windows looked down on Princes Street Gardens, and across the New Town to the Forth.

'Golly, Stephan, how do you get any work done? This is the most amazing view.'

'One gets used to it, fortunately – unfortunately.' Stephan took her coat. 'You must come for a drink some evening. The lights of the city are spectacular.'

'They must be,' Isla said as she continued to gaze at the beautiful city spread out before her eyes.

He laughed at her. 'Come on, if you're good you may sit in the window while we eat our sandwiches.'

Isla sighed. She could not begin to count

the number of times she had looked up from Princes Street or its glorious gardens, to wonder what magical beings lived in those impressive houses up there on the hill. Determined to be more sophisticated, she walked with him to the piano and began.

Stephan was a hard taskmaster, but good at getting the best out of instrumentalists and singers, and soon Isla relaxed. She almost felt regret at going into teacher training instead of the Royal Academy. She now knew how much she had to learn. Still, here she was being coached by Stephan Lenton. How thrilled her mother would be.

And Ross? Isla almost missed her entry as she acknowledged that, possibly for the first time, Ross had not been foremost in her mind. Right now, however, she tried to put him out of her thoughts as she concentrated on the music and on Stephan's instructions.

'You did well today, Madame Diva,' he said later, as they sat looking down on Edinburgh's famous gardens.

Isla felt herself blushing with pride and

embarrassment. 'Thank you.' She avoided looking at him and chose a sandwich from the selection on the plate before them. 'These look delicious.'

'I think you said one of your friends is a caterer?'

'Yes, she works for Fabulous Foods.'

'Lucky you, to have her as a flatmate – she must be good. I was at a wedding that company catered for. The food was absolutely delicious, with beautiful presentation, too. Which is what we'll work on after lunch, if you can spare some more time.'

Isla gulped. 'Of course I can, Stephan. This is extraordinarily kind of you.'

He smiled as he stood up and poured her a glass of fruit juice. 'Not at all. My reputation is at stake here. Besides, little Miss Wren, with a lot of hard work, I do believe we can make a star out of you.'

It was early evening before Isla, a million thoughts chasing themselves round and round in her head, caught a bus that would take her almost directly home. She was exhausted, but at the same time exhilarated. The exhilaration lasted until she became aware of the looming urgency of talking to Ross, who was still expecting her to drive up to see him on Saturday. She had been the one to suggest it, telling him that she wanted – needed – to talk, to work out something. After all, many couples led happy lives even thought they were often far apart.

And now she was about to break the promise she had made to Ross, when she had broken so many promises already.

But that was last week, when missing him had been an ever-present pain. Today, words had been uttered that every young singer waits for. 'I do believe we can make a star out of you.'

Jenny, hoping to meet Simon for coffee, had in fact left the flat long before Holly. But, although he was supposed to be on duty, there was no sign of him. Only the ward sister was there, going over notes.

She looked up and smiled. 'We got a

kidney during the night.'

That explained everything. Jenny's heart raced with happiness for her patient. 'Wonderful; it was Mrs Macleod, wasn't it?' She looked down the ward, but it was impossible to see anything since two of the beds were surrounded by screens.

'It was indeed, and everything went well. She's still down in Recovery, though, and will be for some time.'

The nurses looked at each other with relief and satisfaction. Every patient was special.

'We'll put her into a side room, and then she should be able to see her wee girls in a day or two.'

'Best medicine,' Jenny agreed, and prepared to start her day's work.

Obviously Simon had been a part of the surgical team, so it was unlikely that she would see him today. She saw that she had time to look in on the special patient in the recovery room.

Simon was there, standing beside the bed, looking down at the girl. He turned as the door opened and, on seeing Jenny, his face lit up.

'Jenny.'

She went to him and doctor and nurse stood, hand in hand, while the patient slept.

'It was perfect, Jenny,' he said. 'Text book.'

As much as Simon, Jenny was aware that the transplant patient was not yet out of danger but, just for this moment, they relaxed in a job well done, in the hope of a normal life for a young woman and her family.

Unable to control his fatigue, Simon yawned. 'I've had it, darling,' he said, 'must go. But...' He hesitated for a moment as if unsure of what to say. 'I did a lot of thinking last night, watching this girl. It made me realise I've rushed you into this. We didn't see each other for years and – yes, I know it was my stupid fault. Then we found ourselves together again. Those early days were miserable, but now it's as if we have never been apart. Earlier, in the operating room, I looked at this young woman and I wondered what she wanted out of life, and what she might choose to do, now that she's been given a chance. But it was your face I was seeing.'

A cold feeling in the pit of her stomach, Jenny looked at him. 'What are you trying to say, Simon?'

'It's just, I still worry about whether you really wanted to become a doctor. Yes, I know you said it was your dad's dream. But he was so sure at the time. I don't want you to be like Isla, unhappy and unfulfilled.'

She could hardly believe she was hearing this, and became angry. 'Since when did you become an expert on Isla's feelings?'

Surprised by her unaccustomed vehemence, he reeled back. 'Sorry, but you said she is riddled with guilt. I don't want that for you. I love you, Jenny...'

'Do you?' she whispered fiercely, unhappily aware of the recovering patient in the bed. 'You said that you wanted to marry me, but now you're backing off, just like you did all those years ago in Dumfries. What is it,

Doctor? A case of cold feet?'

Feeling that she was about to burst into very unprofessional tears, she pushed past him and hurried out of the room.

Evelyn's office door was ajar and Holly walked in carrying her tray.

'Why, Holly, you haven't brought enough of that yummy paté for the two of us.'

'I'll eat downstairs, Evelyn. I really want to concentrate on the venison.' She stopped for a moment, then continued. 'And, I'm sorry, but I really don't need to know about Hugh and Regina.'

Holly looked so fierce and, at the same time, unhappy that Evelyn stood up and walked over to her. 'At least sit down and have a cup of coffee with me. This paté will be perfect for the wedding, by the way. You definitely have a future, Holly, if you want it, a future in catering or restaurants. Please, sit down – just for a minute.'

She did so but her whole posture was unbending.

'Holly, I've known Hugh for twenty years; my husband has known him longer. I can tell you he is a thoroughly decent human being. He was in love once, it's true. Everything was perfect until he was sent abroad. Regina just couldn't understand or tolerate the demands the Army made on him. He would make a date with her, only to be a thousand miles away when he was supposed to be at a ball at the Assembly Rooms. He would have to break lunch engagements, dinner dates, concerts, you name it. Regina couldn't stand playing second fiddle.'

Holly stood up, her tea untouched. 'I don't understand why you're telling me all this.'

Evelyn sighed. 'I'm just saying that. For a career soldier, the Army will always come first. I wouldn't want to see you hurt.'

In her room, Isla lay on her bed and relived the day. Every moment in Stephan's flat had been wonderful. For the first time, she had felt like a professional singer. Over and over again she had striven to achieve the effects that Stephan demanded. He spoke in academic terms – of equalising the voice, of head cavities and chest cavities, of the larynx, of fullness of tone, of beauty of sound.

'In this phrase the sound must be flawless, Isla, absolutely flawless.'

She had tried and failed and tried again, had burst into tears – which he had ignored – and had then tried again until at last she had heard the magical words, 'That's more like it.'

Twice they had stopped, once to eat sandwiches and later to drink water. Stephan approved of water. 'No dairy foods for the rest of the week, Isla, plenty of exercise and sleep, and remember to practice as early in the mornings as possible.'

She had stored up all the advice and, mindful of the need for exercise, had walked home. While her heart sang with joy over her new experiences, her mind was busy with the question of what to say to Ross.

She knew she had to ring him but instead she found herself reaching for her copy of 'The Marriage of Figaro'. But she quickly realised that she was making no sense of the words, or of the notes that marched relentlessly up and down and across the pages. She reached for her laptop instead and inserted a disc of the great German soprano, Elisabeth Schwarzkopf, singing the role of the countess in a recording made in Vienna in 1950.

Isla lay back on her pillows and listened to the magical music.

To be able to sing like that. Was it possible that Stephan believed that she could, one day?

She fast-forwarded to listen to the countess dictating a letter to her maid, Susanna, here sung by an equally great singer, Irmgard Seefried. Very quietly she tried to sing along with Susanna, but decided quickly to stop. How to make yourself feel small in one easy lesson.

She started the disc again and this time

she lay back listening, singing Susanna's part in her head. She had just decided that, taking everything into consideration, her performance was not too bad when her mobile rang.

She jumped from the bed and stood, for a breathless moment, looking at it.

Then she took a deep breath, and picked it up.

It was Ross.

Isla had gone over and over in her head how she thought this conversation would go, when she eventually found the courage to talk to him. Now she found her finger-nails painfully digging into the palm of her hand. 'Ross,' she began just as he said, 'Isla.'

'You said you'd let me know when to expect you, Isla. I can't wait to see you.'

He stopped talking, waiting for her to speak.

'Ross.'

'What is it?'

'Something came up, Ross. It's a one off – a chance I just couldn't turn down. I'm going to be singing... Ross, can you hear me? Are you still there?'

There was no reply. He had disconnected.

When Holly reached the flat that evening she saw that the doors of her friends' bedrooms were closed. Not a good sign – usually all three doors remained open so that the friends could call to one another or feel free to pop in to chat.

'I'm having a shower,' she called and, after throwing her coat on her bed and checking that no e-mail had come in from Hugh, cancelling their date, she locked herself in the bathroom and did exactly that. How good it felt. The hot water seemed to wash away all the tensions of the day. After fleeing Evelyn's office she had returned to the kitchen to finish preparing the venison entrée. Had the other chefs been watching her they would have thought there was nothing amiss, but her mind was full of thoughts of Hugh Crawford.

She'd decided that her boss's warning had

been kindly meant. Evelyn knew her friend and accepted his life style, but obviously did not want her newest chef to have her heart broken. Much too early to talk of hearts, though. Holly thought of what her boss had told her. Hugh had loved Regina, who hadn't been able to cope with weeks and months alone. Poor Regina. Poor Hugh. Now, if she were to love a man like Hugh Crawford...

Deliberately stopping her train of thought right there, she'd spent the rest of the day concocting a superb sauce for the venison.

After her shower Holly went to make tea. Neither Isla nor Jenny appeared, but after a while she heard music from Isla's room, surely a good sign. There was still no sound from Jenny's room. Holly went to the door and listened. Could she hear faint sobbing? Without knocking, she Holly turned the handle and went in.

Jenny, still in her uniform, was lying on top of her bed, and she had been crying.

'Oh, Jen.' Holly sat down on the bed and

began to rub Jenny's back. 'What is it, Jenny? Can I help? Would you like a cup of tea?'

There was a reluctant laugh from the figure on the bed, and Jenny sniffed loudly and sat up. 'Holly, you are priceless. A cup of tea fixes everything, is that it?'

'Absolutely. Isla sings. I do tea. Can you tell me what's wrong, or do you want me to leave?'

'Simon doesn't love me.' Jenny began to cry again.

Holly could recognise signs of exhaustion. She waited until Jenny was quiet and then said, 'He does, very much.'

Jenny sat up, reaching for tissues. 'Then explain why he's pushing me away. He says I should study medicine and he doesn't want to hold me back. Oh, Holly, I was so proud of him. He had operated all night on this young woman, and it was a success and I wanted to hug him. But then he suddenly said he didn't want me to be unfulfilled. He's changed his mind about us, I know it.'

Holly frowned. 'Did he say so?'

'Not exactly.' Jenny shredded the tissues in her hand and reached for fresh ones. 'He says he doesn't want me to spend the rest of my life wishing I had done more with it. It's true that I thought once, a long time ago, that I might, want to be a doctor. But it was just a phase. Besides, even if I were to become a medical student, why should that stop us getting married?'

Holly was trying to formulate an answer when she heard a sniff from the doorway and there stood Isla. She, too, had red-rimmed eyes and was clutching a wad of tissues.

'Good grief.' Holly jumped up and rushing over to her. 'Didn't the practice go well?'

Jenny made room for Isla on the bed.

'Misery loves company, they say. Come and tell us all about it. Was it dreadful?'

'It was wonderful.' Isla started to cry again. 'Stephan thinks I'm going to be a star. But I had promised to see Ross on Saturday – we were going to have a good long talk. When I rang him to explain that

I've been asked to sing at the Queen's Hall, he hung up on me. I've called his number a million times, but he won't answer.'

Holly found herself torn between feelings of anger for her brother's sake and pity for her friend. She sighed, but then knew a temptation to giggle. By now a very soggy Jenny and Isla were sitting on the bed, sobbing and sniffing together. No, now was not the time to tell her unhappy friends that she had a date with Hugh.

'This can all be worked out, girls, I'm sure. Jenny, you said that when Simon spoke to you he was exhausted; he'd been operating all night. He probably hasn't been thinking clearly. Yes, of course you could still do your medical training, though between Simon's shifts and yours, you newly-weds might not see very much of each other. Maybe that was in his mind too. But the bottom line is, Simon loves you and you love him. That's all that matters.'

Jenny went to respond, but Holly held up her hand.

'Wait, I'm not finished. I'm going to make a fresh pot of tea because I need it, and while I'm making it, Jenny, you ring Simon. Isla, you are going to sing on Saturday because that is the only way you will know what it is that you do want.'

She left them both looking slightly stunned, and went to the kitchen. The course of true love and all that, she told herself as she filled the kettle. What else could possibly go wrong?'

Episode 6

'Simon loves you. Now go and call him.'

Holly's stern admonition had such a powerful effect on Jenny that she went immediately to her room to phone Simon. She sat down on the edge of her bed for a few minutes and, with her eyes closed, breathed slowly and calmly.

'Right, here goes.' She picked up her mobile phone and pressed his number. Engaged. She tried again. Engaged.

He couldn't be that miserable if he was chatting on the phone, she decided sadly. She tried to tell herself that she did not care, that she would have a hot shower and go to bed. Then the mobile rang in her hand, startling her so much that she dropped it on the white cover.

With trembling hands she picked it up. 'Hello?'

'Jenny, I'm sorry. Oh, darling, please forgive me. I love you; I always have loved you.' He was silent for a moment. 'Jenny, are you there?'

'I love you too, Simon. But I really don't want to be a doctor.'

He laughed shakily. 'I don't care whether you want to be a doctor, an astronaut or to go searching for the lost city of Atlantis – as long as you want to marry me first. I wasn't thinking straight. The pressure of lectures and essays, of being on call, never seeing each other for more than a few minutes each day... I suppose I just panicked that it would be asking too much of you. Jackass that I was, I even imagined that I was doing a fine and noble thing by stepping out of the picture.'

'That's what Holly said,' Jenny admitted. 'But, even if that were the case, I'd still rather go through it all by your side, Simon, than on my own. Even if I won't always be the perfect little wife, with a hot meal ready on the table when you get home.'

He gave a shaky laugh, which betrayed how anguished he had been. 'I don't want the perfect wife – I want you. That is, oh, drat, I know that didn't come out right, but... Jenny, are you laughing at me?' His voice became indignant.

She laughed again.

'Yes. Yes I am. And perhaps that's a good thing. If we had taken ourselves less seriously, talking about our fears instead of making assumptions, we might never have parted.'

'My wise, wonderful Jenny.' His voice was warm and full of love. 'I must go and crash, or I won't be fit for work tomorrow. I'll see you then. Goodnight, my love.'

After he had rung off, Jenny wanted to share her joy. But the flat was dark and quiet, so she went to bed, hugging her happiness to her.

By the next morning Holly had had good news of her own. There had been a message from Hugh.

Wednesday, 8 pm The Outsider.
Hope this suits.
Hugh

Of course it suited. She replied to the e-mail and then, without disturbing the others, went happily off to work. Her good news would keep, and hopefully her flatmates' moods would have improved by the end of the day.

She was surprised to see Samantha Gracie

sitting alone in Evelyn's industrial kitchen.

'A word, Miss Maxwell?'

She gestured with her hand, as if to some menial. Holly put down the bowl in which she had begun to gather ingredients and, moving from her station, she tied on her apron, wondering what on earth this person could have to say to her.

'You may say I have no right to speak to you about your private life...' the older woman began.

Holly nodded. 'No right at all.'

Samantha coloured, but went on. 'I have your best interests at heart, believe me.'

'You know nothing about me, or my best interests. Was there anything else?'

'Evelyn tells me that you are seeing Hugh Crawford next week.'

'Good gracious. It never occurred to me Mrs Hammond would discuss my private life.'

Samantha stood up. 'Silly girl; we're worried about you, and don't want you to be hurt. If Hugh does ever marry,' she said, seeming to pick her words with care, 'he won't be the fool he was ten years ago. He won't be caught again by some naïve girl. This time he will look for a woman who understands military life. It can be difficult, you know. An officer's wife must be prepared to be alone for weeks, even months at a time. Young women can't usually handle that. Could you, Miss Maxwell?'

She's in love with him herself, Holly thought, suddenly understanding, and she sees me as a threat. As calmly as she could, she faced the woman. 'I'm having supper with Major Crawford, Mrs Gracie, not marrying him. But since you ask, if I did love someone I am quite sure I could handle anything.'

Holly turned and walked back to her station, grinning as she heard the sound of retreating high-heeled shoes, and then a distant but obviously heated conversation.

Holly stared into the bowl without seeing the ingredients. Her heart began to lift with joy as, with renewed energy, she stirred the mixture. 'I think I'm falling in love, and I also think – I hope – that he is falling in love with me.'

Bowl in hand, she waltzed around the kitchen, just as the door opened and her employer, looking flustered, entered.

Evelyn looked around almost furtively before speaking. 'Holly, please believe that I had no idea Sam was here. I don't know who let her in and, whatever she says, I did not discuss you with her. Mind you, I did mention in passing, that you would be seeing Hugh some time next week, but only because I was so pleased.'

'I'm fine, Evelyn. Mrs Gracie doesn't bother me.'

A second message from Hugh that evening made her even happier.

Wednesday is a lifetime away. Drat military exercise. I'll make some free time on Sunday and ring you. H

'The show must go on.' A very tired Isla

looked at her face in the bathroom mirror, wincing a little as she saw the dark circles under her eyes. Deliberately she dipped her face in the basin of ice-cold water. She was due at the Queen's Hall in less than an hour for a rehearsal, and she looked and felt terrible.

Having scarcely slept for the past few nights, walking in the Meadows to clear her head had only exhausted her more, as unpleasant thoughts chased each other around in her mind. Not only had Ross refused her calls, but her parents, too, were disappointed.

'The opera's one thing, Isla; that was a commitment. But to accept an invitation, when you had already made an arrangement with Ross, was just bad manners,' her mother had commented on the phone.

No use to explain that to accept had been Isla's instinctive reaction, made without any thought at all.

Even so, you could have cancelled, Isla told her reflection in the mirror.

She looked at her drawn face, put on more make-up than was usual for daytime, and hurried off to the venue.

While Isla was trying to relax and build her confidence, Holly went shopping for a new dress for her date with Hugh, and Jenny and Simon hunted for engagement rings. Both girls hoped that their friend would be feeling well enough to perform.

That evening, Holly, Jenny and Simon arrived early at the Queen's Hall for the evening's gala concert. They couldn't see Isla's parents, which was unusual as the Wrens never missed one of her performances.

'Don't say they're not coming. This is going to be heart-breaking for Isla.' Jenny peered around the audience. 'No Ross. No parents.'

'There's still time,' Holly soothed, 'and if they don't show up, then we'll have to be family enough for her.'

They sat down, and watched as the seats

around them filled up. Just as the orchestra began to warm up, Isla's parents, looking flustered, hurried past them to some empty seats.

The concert started, one item following another until finally Isla walked forward with the conductor. She was pale and, Holly could tell, was trembling. Then the music began.

Holly clasped her hands tightly together as the introduction to one of the loveliest of all soprano arias was heard – 'Mi Chiamano Mimi', from Puccini's glorious opera, 'La Bohème'.

Isla had been nervous about singing this well-known and much-loved aria before an audience who, in all probability, would know it as well as she did. But there was no need to fear. Her lovely voice was touching as she became the seamstress, telling of her dull job. Then the atmosphere changed, and music and voice soared together as the captivated audience heard the young soprano sing of how she longed for spring.

The applause at the end was tumultuous, and Isla's friends hugged each other. This surely was where she belonged.

Thrilled by the response, Isla allowed herself to be led to the front several times to be applauded. She was happy to see her friends there, and threw a look of pure joy as she spotted her parents.

But Ross had not come.

That was it then. He didn't love her any more. Despair threatened to overwhelm her as she returned to her dressing room to wait for the second part of the programme. She had been asked to sing another well-known aria from Verdi's 'Rigoletto'. Isla emerged and sang of Gilda's love for the poor student, Gaultier, but the name that filled her heart and mind was Ross.

Once again, applause rocked the auditorium. As Isla bowed and thanked the orchestra and the conductor; none but her parents and her friends could guess that her heart was breaking.

'I'm driving up to Aberdeen,' she told

them after the performance.

'Whatever happens I will sing in the opera, because I promised. But none of it is worthwhile if Ross isn't behind me.'

'But it's so late,' Mrs Wren fretted. 'Come home with us now, and drive up tomorrow.'

'I can't wait that long. I may have left it too late already, but I have to try.'

'The food's not anything to write home about, though.' Hugh Crawford's warm chuckle came down the phone. 'Couldn't you consider turning your catering talents to Army fare?'

Holly laughed, amazed at how comfortable she felt chatting with him. 'I doubt if the Army could run to smoked salmon and venison, but I'd give it a go.'

It was Sunday morning and, true to his word, Hugh had called her. 'Till Wednesday evening,' he said as they ended their conversation. 'After that, for a few months, at least, life should be fairly normal. I'd like you to see my home in the spring, with

173

thousands of flowers in bloom. It's what I see in my mind when I'm ... working.' He paused for a moment, and then added softly, 'I would love that picture to include you.'

Holly was recalling those precious words, and the warm tone of Hugh's voice, as she stood at her work station on Wednesday morning. She didn't hear Boris come in, and was startled when he spoke to her in a tone quite different from his usual friendly one.

'The boss wants you in her office. You have – what's the expression? – blown it up, Miss Maxwell.'

'What are you talking about, Boris? Blown what?'

He just gave an unpleasant laugh, so she hurried upstairs from the basement kitchens, going over and over her recent assignments, but thinking of nothing that might have annoyed Evelyn.

As she knocked on the office door she heard Evelyn say, 'Come in,' in an angry tone.

'Boris says you want to talk to me, Evelyn.'

'How could you do this to me?'

'I don't know what you're talking about.'

Evelyn stood up. 'Samantha Gracie rang me up just now, to find out what time to expect us tomorrow. It seems we have agreed to prepare supper for her friends – several of whom just happen to be some of my most important clients – after the play at the King's Theatre. She said she arranged it with you. But it's not down here in the book.' She walked to the window. 'I'm disappointed, Holly. I can't believe you would be so careless.'

Holly couldn't believe what she was hearing. 'That's impossible. I did speak to Mrs Gracie, several weeks ago. And I definitely put it in the book.'

Evelyn looked sceptical. 'Then why does it say *Evelyn and Boris demonstration?* See for yourself.'

Holly looked down at the page, already suspecting what she would see. She knew for sure that she had written in the Gracie booking. But Boris's heavy handwriting now filled the space, covering any earlier marks.

She looked at her boss sadly. 'Had I made a mistake, I would have admitted it, Evelyn. Obviously you can't cater for the supper now, but I can. Please ring Mrs Gracie and assure her that the best after-theatre supper she's ever seen will be on her table when she returns with her guests tomorrow evening. Now, if you'll excuse me, I must go and start prepping.'

She walked out, closing the door quietly behind her.

Boris was in the kitchen separating eggs. 'Well, Holly. When you blow you do great. I wish I could help. You got fired, yes?'

Holly looked at Boris. Was she imagining a gleam of triumph in the pastry chef's eyes? Surely he had to have seen her previous note in the book. Then, always ready to give people the benefit of the doubt, Holly chose to believe that he'd scribbled in his own booking quickly, without realizing. Still, he was clearly enjoying her discomfiture.

'Excuse me, Boris, but I have a party to

prepare for.'

She almost laughed aloud at the startled look on his face.

Isla managed to get through to Holly's phone as her friend was approaching the door to their building. Holly stopped to see who the caller was, aware that she was too upset to speak to Evelyn. 'Please don't let it be Hugh either,' she breathed.

Then, seeing who was calling her, she pushed the talk button joyfully.

'Isla, at last. We've been so worried. Are you OK?'

Isla laughed. 'More than OK, Hol. I'm so sorry not to have rung before, but I didn't get to Ross's place until Sunday. It was snowing, so I stopped in a lay-by, assuming I might have to stay there until morning. It was absolutely freezing. I'd left a message on Ross's phone, and he came for me – my wonderful knight ... in a dirty old Land Rover. He brought blankets and hot coffee. Bliss.'

She laughed again. 'Can you begin to imagine what I felt seeing him coming over the hill? He's such a wonderful person, Holly.'

'I know my big brother, Isla Wren,' Holly pointed out, shivering with cold as she stood there in the street. If she went into the building she might lose the connection, so she had to stay where she was while the wind blew around her. 'Go on, what happened next?'

'We left my car there, and he drove me to the farm. We were both exhausted, but we talked for hours, and finally ... well, everything's fine again. I'm at Mum and Dad's right now. They came up yesterday and I followed them back down.'

'And the wedding?'

'We haven't looked that far ahead. But Ross does want me to sing in the opera. Is it OK if I come back to the flat tomorrow?'

Holly's heart sank a little. What if it started all over again, this struggle between being farmer's wife or opera singer?

Isla seemed to guess what she was thinking. 'Don't worry, Holly. We're going to get it right this time, I promise. I'll tell you everything when I get back. Give Jenny the good news, will you?'

'And my parents?'

'They know already. We rang them on Sunday, just after we spoke to my mum and dad. Forgive us for not calling you, but we needed that time together. You understand, don't you?'

Holly smiled. 'Yes, of course. I'm so happy for you both.'

'What about Jenny? Did she choose a ring?'

'Simon chose it for her. A lovely emerald.'

'Can't wait to see you,' Isla retorted, and hung up.

Holly climbed upstairs to the flat, marvelling at how swiftly things had changed. Tomorrow Isla would be returning, but for how long? Jenny and Simon were bound to marry soon, both agreeing that enough time had been wasted already, and so Jenny would be leaving. That would leave Holly Maxwell – a possibly jobless Holly Maxwell – alone, in a flat which she could not afford to keep.

Ross Maxwell had just finished feeding his in-lamb ewes, and was sitting down in front of his Aga with a nice hot cup of soup. He looked across at the chair where Isla had sat, curled up in blankets, early on Sunday morning, and he smiled.

She was back. His Isla was back. He dialled her number. 'Hi, how are you?'

'Missing you.'

'That's what I wanted to hear. What did our Holly have to say?'

'I did most of the talking, but she's taking me back.'

'I knew she would. Holly's your friend, Isla, and very soon she'll be your sister-in-law, too.'

Each was quiet for a moment, then Ross spoke. 'When are you leaving for Edinburgh?'

'Soon as Dad comes home.'

'Ring me when you get there. Isla, will you marry me?'

'Ross, I thought we had agreed to all that.'

'Yes, but I mean will you marry me now, Isla, just as soon as it can be arranged. I'll follow you anywhere and no one will be cheering louder than me. Just do me one favour. Try to schedule your concerts outside lambing.'

Holly rang the hospital and left a message for Jenny, who would be delighted to learn that, for Isla too, there was to be a happy ending.

Far too early for her date with Hugh, she had styled her hair and then changed her mind several times until, wearing the dress bought specially for the occasion, she set off for the restaurant.

The Edinburgh taxi driver had no difficulty in finding The Outsider, the restaurant on George IV Bridge where she was to meet Hugh. Despite her jangling nerves, Holly was pleased to be there, as this restaurant was on her list of restaurants to sample. If she were to start out on her own

She abandoned that train of thought. Tonight was not the time to think about business. Just for now she would give herself up to the pleasure of thinking about Major Hugh Crawford.

He hadn't yet arrived at the restaurant, but she was shown to the table that had been reserved for him. Right away, she knew that it was one of the best in the establishment. Not only was it possible to watch fellow diners without overhearing their conversations, but the table was beside a window which seemed to frame the incredible beauty and majesty of Edinburgh Castle.

'Wow,' she said, sinking into her comfortable chair.

The waiter smiled. 'May I get you anything?'

'I'll wait, thanks.' said Holly

He smiled again and withdrew.

She was about to check her lipstick when she felt, rather than saw, Hugh enter the restaurant. She had expected, for some reason, that he would be in uniform, but he had had time to change. Nevertheless, he still looked like a soldier. He was tall and broad, like many men, but there was an air about him that was dynamic and exciting.

'Holly.' He kissed her easily on the cheek. 'Forgive me for being late.'

Not having expected the kiss, she felt butterflies riot once more in her stomach, and had to force her hand not to reach up to touch her face. 'Not at all. I enjoyed looking at the castle,' she said, and was surprised by how normal her voice sounded.

He raised his hand towards the waiter, who was standing by the desk. 'I hope you're hungry, Holly. Now, shall we have some wine?'

Later, Holly found it impossible to remember the taste of anything. What she did recall was that everything was quite delicious and beautifully presented.

She had decided not to mention her rift at work to Hugh, who was, after all, a close friend of Evelyn, and conversation flowed easily. Holly was interested in hearing as much about his work as Hugh was prepared to tell. He chose his anecdotes carefully – funny stories, sad stories, and stories of bravery.

She, in turn, made him smile when she told him all about her childhood on the family farm, of her years in France, her experience in great French restaurants and even of her long-ago French boyfriend.

Growing up as a privileged only son in an ancient castle had been a very different experience, he informed her. Happy, but lonely nonetheless. 'You were lucky you to have an older brother, Holly. I asked my parents for one every Christmas – well, at least until I was six.' He smiled. 'But I had my dogs, spaniels, a deerhound – which I wanted to take him to school with me – and Labradors of course. What about you?'

'It's different on a farm, Hugh. We love our sheepdogs but they're more working dogs than family pets. And then, for company I always had Jenny and Isla who were like my sisters.'

'That's nice. Mind you, in one way, I have had lots of brothers.'

His face looked sombre for a moment, and Holly remembered that his best friend had died in combat. She reached out, and he smiled at her and gripped her hand for a moment.

Just then the maitre d' approached the table. 'Major Crawford? There's a call for you at the desk.'

Hugh stood up. 'Dash it. I thought I'd be able to have at least one uninterrupted evening. Forgive me, Holly, I'll be right back.'

He ordered coffee to be brought to the table and moved off. Holly was delighted and more than a little amused to see how many other women watched his progress through the tables.

She was pouring coffee when he came back and sat down. 'Life is so full of unnecessary complications, isn't it?'

'Was the call to do with your work?'

'No, with yours.' He looked grim. 'That was Evelyn. She knew I'd pick this place. Holly, I'm so sorry Sam has been such a nuisance. I want you to know that I have never encouraged her to believe that I care for her. At least, not in the way I've begun to care for you.'

Holly lowered her head, her breath quickening.

'Evelyn wanted you to know she's very sorry, Holly. She's terrified that you'll leave her now.'

'I haven't decided what to do next, yet, and I wish she hadn't got in touch with you.' With eyes that pricked from tears she forced not to fall, she looked at him. 'Trust is important to me, Hugh, and Evelyn clearly doesn't trust me.' She shrugged. 'I know that Mrs Gracie made the booking, and I know that I wrote it in the book. What made me angry is that Evelyn immediately assumed I had been unprofessional.'

'I think I understand. But isn't she allowed one error in judgement? Evelyn isn't your enemy, and she's very fond of you. She also knows what effect you have on me.'

Aware of his tanned fingers against her white hand, she managed a smile. 'We'll see. I've put together a menu, and tomorrow morning I will go in early and prepare it. Evelyn will be engaged tomorrow evening, of course, as will Boris, so I'll have to take the food to Mrs Gracie's house and serve it myself.'

'Want an assistant?' His face was perfectly serious. 'I'll be free tomorrow evening. I'd be happy to stay in the kitchen and chop carrots, wash dishes ... you name it. You have no idea how versatile we soldiers are.'

In spite of herself, Holly laughed. 'Major Crawford, washing up?'

'You've seen my ancient kitchen – you must know I'm a dab hand at washing up.'

How she longed to accept his offer, however lightly made. She stood up. 'Thank you, but I'll manage. I'd best get home, Hugh. Lots to do tomorrow.'

'Wait, Holly. There's something I haven't

told you yet. It's about my next assignment. I'm going out to Afghanistan in June, and I'll be gone for at least six months.'

Hugh helped Holly on with her coat, and she waited as he paid the bill. Then they walked in silence out of the restaurant.

He was a good driver, and it seemed to take no time at all to drive through one of the most historical parts of Edinburgh. But, for once, Holly was unaware of the beauty around her. The realization that he would be leaving again so soon had shaken her. But then, was this not precisely what both Evelyn and Samantha had warned her about? So was she really going to fall at the first hurdle?

They reached her building, and he insisted on seeing her to the door of her flat. 'Holly, whatever you decide regarding working with Evelyn, it makes no odds to me. You've become very important to me. I just hope you're not put off by the news of my posting.'

He seized her hands urgently, his voice

throbbing and passionate. The soldier was gone, and here was just a man. 'What I mean is ... I love you. It's wonderful. I never expected to find love again. I could face anything, if I knew you'd be waiting for me when I returned.'

She looked up into his anxious eyes, her heart singing at his declaration of love. 'I love you too, Hugh.'

His lips touched hers so lightly that she felt that she could almost have imagined it. Then he turned and ran down the staircase.

It was turning out to be another fine June day. Holly, Isla and Jenny stood on the tarmac at Brize Norton. Their heads were tilted up into the sky, watching a great grey bird streaking away. The plane was carrying all of Holly's hopes, and Holly's future happiness. She knew that Hugh could not possibly see her, but she raised her hand and waved anyway. The sunlight caused the diamonds in the antique ring on her left hand to sparkle.

He would come back, she knew it. He would come back. And she would be waiting.

Linking arms with her two best friends in the world, Holly managed to smile as they walked towards the staff car that was waiting to take them to the station.

'Come on,' she said. 'With luck, we'll be back in Edinburgh in time for dinner.'

The publishers hope that this book has given you enjoyable reading. Large Print Books are especially designed to be as easy to see and hold as possible. If you wish a complete list of our books please ask at your local library or write directly to:

Dales Large Print Books
Magna House, Long Preston,
Skipton, North Yorkshire.
BD23 4ND